SOMETHING DEADLY THIS WAY COMES

Also by KIM HARRISON:

ONCE DEAD, TWICE SHY

EARLY TO DEATH, EARLY TO RISE

SOMETHING DEADLY THIS WAY COMES

A NOVEL

KIM HARRISON

HARPER
An Imprint of HarperCollinsPublishers

Library of Congress Cataloging-in-Publication Data

Harrison, Kim.

Something deadly this way comes / Kim Harrison. — 1st ed.

p. cm.

Summary: Technically dead seventeen-year-old Madison must choose between reclaiming her body and continuing as dark timekeeper, struggling in the war between light and dark reapers while trying to change the rules.

ISBN 978-0-06-171819-9

[1. Dead—Fiction. 2. Death—Fiction. 3. Future life—Fiction. 4. Fate and fatalism—Fiction. 5. Supernatural—Fiction. 6. Fantasy.] I. Title.

PZ7.H2526Som 2011   2010027754

[Fic]—dc22   CIP

                                                                    AC

Typography by David Caplan

11 12 13 14 15   CG/RRDB   10 9 8 7 6 5 4 3 2 1

First Edition

SOMETHING DEADLY THIS WAY COMES

PROLOGUE

I'm Madison Avery, dark timekeeper in charge of heaven's hit squad . . . and fighting it all the way. Funny how timekeeper never popped up on my "careers good for you" when I did the test at school. The seraphs say I was born to the position, and when the choice was take the job or die? Well . . . I took the job.

"Fate," the seraphs would say. "Bad choice" if you ask me. Even now I don't believe in fate, and so I'm stuck working with a confused dark reaper who is trying to understand, and a light reaper twice fallen from heaven who thinks my ideas are a lost cause. Instead of just following orders sent down from above, I want to do things my own way, which involves trying to convince people to change. My only hope is to locate my real body so I can give the amulet back and forget the entire thing happened, because convincing heaven that I can save lost souls is looking impossible. It'd be a lot easier if my own people weren't working against me.

ONE

The hot sun seemed to go right through me, reflecting off the aluminum bleachers to warm me from my feet up as I stood beside Nakita and cheered Josh on. He was running the two-mile in an invitational, and they were doing the last bit right on the track. The front three runners had begun to pick up the pace for the last hundred yards. Josh was ahead, but the guy behind him had saved some push for the last bit, too.

"Go, Josh! Run! Run!" Nakita yelled, and surprised, I lowered my camera to look at her. The dark reaper didn't especially like Josh—she'd almost killed him once—and her excitement was unusual. Her pale face was flushed, and her eyes, usually a faded blue, were bright as she leaned forward and grasped the chain-link fence between us and the track. She was wearing a pink top with matching pink nail polish to hide her naturally black nails. Open-toed sandals and capris helped her blend in, and she looked nothing like one might imagine a dark reaper, capable of "smiting" lost souls.

I was dressing down today—at least for me—in jeans and a black, lacy top. My hair, though, was its usual purple-tipped cut, hanging around my ears, and I still wore my funky yellow sneakers with their new black laces with skulls on them. They matched my earrings.

"He's right behind you!" the angel in disguise shouted, and her matte-black amulet sparked violet at its core. More evidence she was excited. Shaking my head, I turned back to the race, bringing my camera up and focusing on the finish line. I snapped a picture for the school paper as Josh squeaked over the finish line. My smile was full of a quiet satisfaction that he'd won.

"He won! He won!" Nakita exclaimed, and I gasped when she pulled me into jumping up and down with her. I couldn't help but give her a hug back, breathless as I caught my balance. She certainly wasn't *acting* like one of heaven's hit squad, as excited as if she was Josh's girlfriend. Which she wasn't. I might be. Maybe.

"Barnabas." Nakita shoved his feet where he reclined two rows above us. "Josh won. Say something!"

The former light reaper pushed his hat up and gave her a dry look. "Whoopee," he said sarcastically, then pulled his long legs closer and sat up, squinting in the sun. "Madison, you were going to work with me today on hiding your amulet's resonance."

Grimacing, I looked down at the jet-black stone cradled by silver wires that I wore around my neck. Besides giving me the tactile illusion of a make-believe body, hiding me from black wings, and giving me my connection to the divine, my amulet sang. Sort of. Mimicking a natural aura, the black stone rang like a bell that only the divine could hear. Anyone who knew how to listen could find me in a second—be they friend or foe. Which might be a problem if I was out trying to keep my own people from killing someone, and which was why I needed to learn how to hide it. After hanging out with Josh, of course.

"She can do that later," Nakita said primly. "He won!"

I felt a twinge of guilt. I *had* promised to work with him after school, but I'd forgotten I'd also promised Ms. Cartwright I'd take pictures of the track meet for the school paper.

"Sorry," I said softly, and he shrugged, making no effort to hide his boredom.

For all his sour attitude, Barnabas had been on earth longer than Nakita and therefore had all the subtle nuances of human behavior to fit in with the track moms and cheering girlfriends better than Nakita. His lanky build and faded T-shirt only added to his sigh-worthy looks, but Barnabas truly didn't have a clue how good he looked. Nakita didn't know why guys followed her around looking for dates, either. That the two of them hung out with me had the popular cliques cross-eyed.

3

"This was his only race," I offered hesitantly, and Barnabas leaned back, stretching out on the warm bleacher to put his hat over his face.

Turning back to the track, I snapped a picture of Josh as he accepted the congratulations of his teammates. Sweat made patterns on his shirt, and his blond hair was dark with it. He was the only one apart from Barnabas and Nakita who knew I was technically dead; not only had he been there as I had died, but he had held my hand during the whole thing. Yep, I was dead: no heartbeat unless I got excited or scared, no need to eat—though I could do it in a pinch to fit in, and I hadn't had so much as a nap in months. It had been fun at first, but now I'd give just about anything to enjoy a juicy hamburger and crispy fries. Everything sort of tasted like rice cakes.

"I didn't know you liked sports," I said to Nakita as Josh waited for the runners to pass before crossing the track to talk to us through the fence.

"We have contests," she said. "This has the same appeal." Her gaze went from the runners to the moms chatting among themselves, barely conscious of the meet at all. "I came in third once, with the blade," she added.

Barnabas snickered, his face still hidden under his hat. "Real good with that scythe, eh?" he muttered, and she smacked his foot.

"And where did you place?" she asked him hotly.

Sitting up, Barnabas watched Josh, his eyes not seeing him

but the past. "They didn't have contests when I was in heaven."

I winced. Barnabas had been kicked out of heaven before the pyramids had been built.

"Sorry," Nakita said, surprising me with her downcast eyes. She usually took every opportunity to needle Barnabas about his fallen status. According to Nakita, Barnabas had been kicked out of heaven because he'd fallen in love with a human girl.

"Hi, Josh," I said as he scuffed to a halt behind the chain-link fence.

"Almost lost that one," he said, breathing heavily. When he smiled at me, I felt warm inside. We'd been dating for a while, and his smile still hit me hard. And his kisses, even more.

"But you didn't," Nakita said, back to her serious self again. "It was a good run."

Josh gave her a quizzical look, probably wondering at her earnest expression. "Thanks," he said, then wiped the sweat from his neck. I hadn't sweated in months. Not since I'd died.

"Is that your last race?" I asked, already knowing.

"Yup." Josh waved to the guy calling him from the finish line. "I gotta go, but do you want to go to The Low D with me later?" The Low D was the local hangout, short for The Lowest Common Denominator. Three Rivers was a college town, and the students got the joke even if no one else did. His eyes rose to take in Nakita and Barnabas. "All of you?" he added somewhat sourly.

It was hard to find the time to be alone with Josh between school, my dad, my job at the flower shop, and don't forget being the dark timekeeper, stealing every free moment of my day and night. One might think that not needing to sleep would give you tons of time, but it didn't.

Already guessing my answer, Barnabas sighed from under his hat. It was likely going to be after sundown before I practiced shielding my amulet's resonance. But a quiver went through me, and my heart, or at least the memory of it, gave a hard thump and went still. "Sure," I said, smiling. Small word, heavy in significance.

Josh stuck his fingers through the mesh, and I touched them. Josh and I had been through a lot together, especially considering our rocky start when I was his pity date at prom. We were doing good now, even with the dark timekeeper stuff butting in. Smiling with half his face and looking charmingly beguiling, Josh pulled back, finally turning to face his friends as he walked away. Nakita was scowling when I turned around.

"You promised Barnabas you'd practice," she said, surprising me.

"It's okay to put off practice to watch Josh run, but it's not okay if I want to socialize a little?" I asked.

"Absolutely."

It was reaper logic, and I knew I couldn't win. Sad thing was, she was probably right. Turning away, I sat on the bleachers to wait for Josh. Barnabas was behind me smelling of feathers and the back of clouds—and yes, the back of clouds do have a smell. Ignoring me, Nakita went to stand at the fence, watching the stragglers come in. I wondered if she ought to go out for cross-country, then squashed the idea. She was here to protect me from myself, not learn how to run the two-mile.

But all thoughts of practice and The Low D left me when, without warning, a blue ink seemed to pour from the sun, hitting the earth and boiling up like smoke. It bled across the ground, washing over people oblivious to it, turning me cold. In the time it took to pull my head up, the blue had risen to encompass everything.

Puppy presents on the rug. I'm going to flash forward.

My heart gave a pound and stopped as a quick wash of fear slid into me. The last time I'd flashed forward to see the future, I had cried at the stars and felt like I was going to die. Then I fell into someone else's mind and lived out the ugly moment when they began to kill their own soul. That had been almost a month ago, and I didn't know what scared me more: that I might have to live through that hell again, or that the seraphs were giving me another chance to prove that killing a person wasn't necessary to save their soul—and I might screw it up?

According to Grace—my annoying, often missing guardian angel and heavenly liaison—although the seraphs didn't cause my flash forwards, they could stop them or make them come early, sort of screen them to make my transition to a fully functioning dark timekeeper easier. It wasn't like I had a real teacher, having been dumped into the position. You'd think that the seraphs themselves would take on the job of assigning reaps permanently, but apparently angels had a hard time figuring out what was now, what was then, and what was to be, and it took a human to understand time. I happened to be in charge of the bad guys, the ones who killed people before they killed their souls. I'd rather be in charge of the light, who tried to stop the killing, but that's not what had happened.

Voices faded in and out through the blue mist as I waited for the future to take me. "Madison, you can practice at The Low D," Nakita said, kicking the fence to make it shudder. "The distraction will be good. Barnabas, it's no wonder she never learns anything with you, teaching her at midnight on her roof."

I clutched at my knees, terrified that if I moved, I'd find myself convulsing on the ground. The moment when a soul begins to die is traumatic, and it rings through the time lines and into the future, causing the flash forwards. The deeper into the future, the hazier the vision is, ranging from a crystal clarity to a murky nothing that only voices could penetrate. Which meant that if I was the first timekeeper to flash forward I didn't necessarily have the advantage. Ron, the light timekeeper, might flash later, but clearer, and pull the reap right out from under me.

"Guys?" I whispered, and then gasped when the entire track with its runners, coaches, and blue lawn chairs was suddenly superimposed with a scene that was possibly a hundred miles distant and probably days into the future. And though I clutched at the ribbed heat of the aluminum bench, I also stood on a chalk-decorated sidewalk, staring at a three-story apartment building with old cars out front and a busy road behind me, traffic at a standstill. There was fuzzy blue haze at the edges of my vision and around every person, like a second aura.

The night was an awful mix of orange and black as the building burned, flames leaping high to show clusters of neighbors huddled together, dogs barking, and people screaming. Fire trucks spewed air scented with diesel fuel to the curb, which billowed up and warmed my ankles. Roaring. Everything was roaring. And then I realized it was the blood in my head as heartache gripped me.

Johnny is still in there.

The thought echoed in our shared mind. Terror that belonged to the girl whose body I was in filled me, and I felt myself stand, wobbling on the bleachers. I was flashing forward, living someone else's nightmare. This was when her soul started to die, when something so bad happened that she forgot how to live. I was the only one who might be able to save her.

"Johnny!" I shouted, and Nakita turned to me. I could see her shock, and the image of a burning building grew behind her and melted into the reality of the track meet.

"She's flashing," I heard Barnabas say, and his hand clamped over my arm, keeping me from running forward as the girl whose mind I was in bolted.

In my vision, I ran through the cars, dodging firefighters trying to stop me, the blue haze rising from people like a fog. In reality, I felt my heart pound as I locked my knees and swayed so I wouldn't run as well. *I left Johnny alone. He was asleep. I waited until he was asleep after Mom left for work. Oh, God. Mom is going to kill me when she finds out! I don't understand. How can there be a fire?!*

"Johnny!" I whispered as the girl screamed, then jumped when a heavy hand clamped onto my arm, and both the girl and I turned.

I blinked, wavering when I saw Barnabas behind the frightening image of a fireman in full gear, his breath hissing as he tried to keep me from going in. The crowd in the bleachers was standing, cheering on the last of the runners fighting it out. In my vision, the fire screamed, a surreal counterpoint to the terror filling me. Barnabas's hand was on my arm, and he peered at me in sympathy.

"Johnny is in there!" I said, and the fireman stared, his expression hidden behind the face mask. "Let me go. Let me go! I have to get in there!"

As one, the girl and I twisted in Barnabas's/the fireman's grip, and as one, we were hoisted into their arms. I tried not to fight, knowing it wasn't real, but the girl's terror was mine.

I had no heart to beat in my solid, make-believe body, but memory is a funny thing, and I felt the echo of a pulse as Barnabas carried me, taking the jarring steps down the bleachers and to the cooler shade below. The night bathed my heated cheeks, scorched by sun and fire as Barnabas set me on the ground, and the blue haze that clouded the image of the distant future billowed from the fireman, but not the angel. "I'm sorry," both Barnabas and the fireman said, for two different reasons.

Behind the fireman, I could see an ambulance. The lights were off and I felt my life end when they put a small, covered body into it. The sheet was pulled over it all the way. For an instant, she didn't know what that meant, but I'd been in a body bag before, and somehow, when nothing I was thinking could reach her, this did.

"Oh, Johnny!" we sobbed as the reality hit her. In my vision, I started to cry as I watched the flames eat the roof of my room, but my tears were for Johnny. He was gone, and I cried for both Johnny and his sister as I had a vision of his round face and Transformer pajamas. He'd had fish sticks for dinner. I had been so mean, eating the last one when I knew he wanted it.

"I'm so sorry. I'm so sorry," I sobbed, my throat tight as I hunched against the bleacher support/side of the fire truck. Nearby was a fireman, giving me half his attention so I wouldn't run away. Nakita was superimposed on him, making sure no one came close enough to know what was going on. Behind her, the blue sun shone down on the track meet. They were preparing to set up the next race amid the blaring of loudspeakers and the honking of trucks as a new water tanker came in. My brother was dead. It was my fault. I shouldn't have left him alone.

I got up, or at least I did in my vision. I was starting to find the way to dissociate myself from it so I could just watch, making the heartache in the girl easier to bear. Barnabas holding me might have had something to do with it, too.

My fingers traced the name of the city on the fire truck: BAXTER, CA. My gaze rose and I saw the street sign: CORAL WAY. My heart pounded as I realized I had some control of this memory that had yet to be lived.

"Here you go, Tammy," a smoke-smudged man said, draping a blanket smelling of too much fabric softener over my shoulders. I shivered, unable to speak, but I had a name now, and that would help. "Your mom is coming," he added, and Tammy's panic slid through me anew.

Oh, God. Mom. I turned to the fire in a panic. I wanted to undo this, but I couldn't. Johnny was dead. It should be me there, not him. Not him!

"Madison?" Nakita said, and I blinked at the man as his features melted into hers. "Are you all right?"

I had to run away, leave. Facing this was too awful, and the guilt made it hard to breathe. *I should be dead, not Johnny. He was my brother, and now he is dead. Because of me. It should have been me. It should have been me!*

"Madison!"

Barnabas was calling my name, and I gasped as the two realities—one real, one yet to be lived—clashed violently. The blue tint flashed red, and then the future vanished.

The echo of my heart pounded, and I stilled it as I stared up at Barnabas, Nakita, and . . . Josh. Above me, people cheered the last runner to cross the line. It was over. I had flashed into someone else, lived the foretold death-strike of her soul, and . . . survived.

I swayed, trying to shake the guilt and heartache over the girl's brother's death. Tammy. Her name was Tammy. Her belief that she caused her brother's death still rang in me, a despair so heavy that it crushed all else and denied her soul the love it needed to survive. She would run, mentally if not physically, from those who would help her live again, and her soul . . . would wither and die long before her body did. Fate, the seraphs called it, but I didn't believe in fate.

The old dark timekeeper, Kairos, would have sent Nakita to kill Tammy without a thought, taking her soul to save it at the expense of her life. Ron, the current light timekeeper, would, in turn, send a light reaper to stop the scything, saving her life at the cost of her soul, gambling that she would somehow learn to live again. But I wasn't the old dark timekeeper, and I was going to use the opportunity to prove to the seraphs that fate could be sidestepped and we could save her life as well as her soul. All we needed to do was show Tammy a different choice.

Smiling weakly, I extended my hand. Josh took it, pulling me to my feet. I brushed off my butt and shivered in the shade.

I gazed across the track, remembering the vision of billowing smoke and fire leaping as if it was a living thing. Silent, they waited.

I looked at them, seeing Barnabas's knowing resignation that this was not going to be as easy as I wanted it to be, Nakita's fear that I was going to ask her to do something she didn't understand, and Josh's eagerness to do something, anything, different.

"You guys up for a field trip?" I asked.

As one, they all exhaled, Josh grinning widely. "And how!"

TWO

The gravestone I was standing behind came up to my chest, and I rested my arms across the top. The dry, hot breeze shifted the purple tips of my short hair in and out of my eyes as I waited for Barnabas to come back from his on-foot reconnaissance. Nakita was taking shots of the tombstones with her camera, always ready in her little red purse. And Josh was trying to keep from throwing up after his first angel-assisted flight.

Nakita insisted she'd chosen to land in this graveyard because the school was directly across the busy street, but I thought that it might be a dry sense of humor developing in the otherwise humor-deficient and deadly dark reaper. I'd admit the grave-yard was probably a better choice than the fast-food place next door—especially with Josh still hyperventilating.

I glanced at Josh's hunched, shaky outline as he leaned

against a nearby grave marker, his gym bag at his feet and his back to me as he recovered. It probably hadn't helped that we hadn't just been flying, but flinging, as well. The awful nothingness of traveling between space was frightening at best, and the first time Nakita had wrapped her wings around me and flung us from Indiana to a Greek island on the other side of the earth had been awful. I suppose Kairos's island was mine now, since I had his job and he was dead.

But whether we were there to give Josh a chance to catch his breath, or because of Nakita's idea of a joke, the graveyard was quiet and out of the way, with a good view of the buses lining up on the far right—car pickup on the left. We'd crossed a couple of state lines to get here, and it was only three in the afternoon. School was just now letting out.

Smelling lightly of sweat and tennis shoes, Josh wobbled his way over to me. I gave him a smile and shifted down to make room, and together we leaned on the stone, our elbows touching. I was glad he was here.

"Do you see her?" he asked, his blue eyes finally starting to show his excitement.

"No," I said, mentally thanking Beatrice, whose stone we were leaning on. "I never saw Tammy's face. I figured I was lucky to see the name of the town and her street and that the fireman knew her name. But I'm sure she's in there."

I indicated the school with my chin, and he eyed me. "Your timekeeper-sense tingling, eh?" he kidded me, and I gave him an embarrassed look.

"Uh, yeah, actually," I said, not wanting to admit that I'd felt an odd sort of shiver through my aura when we had flown over the school. The same thing had happened on my last prevention, and I was going to trust it this time.

"So how are we going to find her?" Josh asked, watching the kids just now starting to file out in threes and sixes.

Nakita, who was taking sideways pictures of a pollution-stained statue, dark with smoke and mold, said, without looking at me, "I could find her with a street address and a description of her aura, but if you flashed forward, then Ron probably has, too. We need to move fast before he puts a guardian angel on her and we can't do anything."

"We have at least a day," I said, and Nakita looked at me from around her camera. "The flash forward was fuzzy around the edges," I explained. "You only get the clear visions when it's just hours ahead." Grimacing, I looked from her to the school. "I think the seraphs sent this one to me early, knowing I'm not good at this yet."

Though why they wanted to help me was a mystery. Maybe they didn't like Ron, my timekeeper opposite. I knew I didn't. Or maybe they hoped that once I got better at this that I'd start to believe in fate, not free will. Whatever the reason, I was sure that we were at least a day ahead of Ron's natural, seraph-unassisted flash forward, and I wasn't going to squander it.

Nakita glanced at Barnabas, and when he shrugged, she

looked at the school through the lens, snapping a few shots. "The school is still the best place to look," she said. "Standard reap stuff. Go where the humans are." The shutter clicked, and she straightened, frowning at the back of the camera. One of her pictures in our school's expo at the mall had won top honors, and Nakita had been taking shots ever since.

Ron, I thought, scuffing my yellow sneakers against the stone and wishing the annoying man would ignore me like most adults did. Ron worked for the light instead of the dark, and though we both believed in the same thing—that choice was stronger than heaven's fate—he'd rather slap a guardian angel on someone than try to get to the root of the problem and change their life. Which was *exactly* why I was causing trouble with the seraphs, God's muckety-muck high angels, and trying to change things. Even after having already saved one person's life *and* soul, I knew no one but Barnabas believed I really had a chance. And most times, I wondered about Barnabas.

"If we can't find her here, we'll just go to her apartment and wait," I said, scanning the skies past the shifting leaves for black wings. The mindless, dripping sheets of black always seemed to congregate when a scything was about to occur in the hopes of snitching a bit of unattended soul—which sometimes made me wonder if the creepy things could read the time lines as well as a timekeeper. Dark reapers on the hunt brought them in faster than crows on carrion. That they weren't here was a good omen. I hadn't seen one in months, partly because Nakita hid her resonance much of the time, and partly because she wasn't hunting.

Josh turned to sit with his back to the stone. Digging in his gym bag, he brought out his phone. "I'm going to text my mom. Tell her I'll be home later. If anyone asks, I'm with you."

I looked at my watch and added two hours. "Good idea. Where are we supposed to be? The Low D?" Okay, so I lied to my dad. I didn't feel that good about it, but he wasn't going to believe I was somewhere in California, much less dead and trying to change heaven's policy on culling lost souls.

The soft scent of feathers drew my attention, and I smiled as Barnabas strode across the graveyard, hands in his pockets and eyes roving.

"No light reapers, no black wings, and no Grace," he said, running a hand over his frizzy, loosely curling hair and squinting at the buses. "You want me to go check Tammy's apartment?"

No Grace? I couldn't help but wonder why he'd brought Grace into question, but I nodded, glancing at Nakita as the snap on her purse clicked shut. She'd put her camera away, refusing to let Barnabas be involved in anything she wasn't. "You remember the address?" I asked.

"Coral Way," he said, then touched the top of my hand. *I'll come back and tell you if she's there,* echoed in my thoughts, and I jumped. Blinking, I stared at him. Nakita had been shielding my resonance since leaving Three Rivers so Ron wouldn't know where we were if he checked up on us, and I hadn't known it was possible to touch thoughts while shielded. But Barnabas *had* been touching me physically, so maybe that's how he was able to bypass the shield.

"Hey!" Nakita said, eyes flashing a divine silver for an instant. "No passing notes."

Josh closed his phone and looked up at us in question.

"Relax," Barnabas said sourly as his fingers slipped from the top of my hand. "I was just making sure that it was possible." He paused, then said, "See? She didn't hear *that*."

"Because I'm shielded," I said, and Barnabas nodded, his gaze across the street and on the cars lining up. I figured his sudden sour mood wasn't coming from Nakita's mistrust but from his ability to talk to me silently at all. It meant he wasn't a light reaper anymore. He was moving toward the dark side, toward me. That a light reaper had abandoned his millennium-long beliefs to follow me into the enemy camp was a sobering thought. If I could get Nakita and him to work together to save a marked person's body *and* soul, then I might be able to convince the seraphs to do things my way, and the early scythings would stop for good. If, if, if. And if I couldn't, then as soon as I found my body, hidden somewhere between the now and the next, I was giving up my amulet and going back to being normal, alive, and knowing nothing about reapers, timekeepers, and guardian angels.

But the thought lacked the thrill that it once had. I wanted this to work. Bad.

Josh got to his feet, his gym bag in hand, shifting awkwardly at the tension between Nakita and Barnabas. "Hey, um, I'm going to go behind the mausoleum and change, okay? I'll be right back." He turned and walked away to the small building nearby, gray with age and neglect. I watched him go, thinking he looked good. Confident.

Two kids passed him on their bikes, cutting through the cemetery as a shortcut. School was out, and I turned back to the buses, hearing kids yelling at each other. Beside me, Nakita fidgeted. I was starting to feel the tension, too, and I leaned back from the grave marker, brushing the bits of old stone off my shirt as I looked for black wings.

This felt like a real reap. I had flashed forward. I had found the place. I was *trying* to find the mark. If I wasted my head start, a light reaper would show up to stop me. It didn't matter that our goals were the same—save the mark's life—because if I couldn't, Nakita would be there to kill Tammy. Sacrifice the body to save the soul. It was a sucky reason to die.

"Barnabas," I said, still wondering about Grace. "Do you think I should call Grace?" I liked Grace, but she was my contact with the seraphs, and if she wasn't here, it might mean they wanted to see if I could do this without her help. She was too close to the divine for me to see more than the glow of her wings most of the time. Nakita, Barnabas, and I could hear her chimelike voice, but no one else could. Grace thought she was a poet. Which might be why Josh seemed to be the only one glad when she was around.

"I wouldn't," Barnabas said, his expression closed and worrying me all the more. "I'll go check the apartment."

"Thanks," I said softly, and he walked away to find a quiet place to find his wings, and then, the air.

"I thought he'd never leave," Nakita said.

"Oh, come on," I coaxed, walking backward to the high fence between us and the street. "Barnabas is okay. Admit that you're mad he's turning into a dark reaper, and get over it."

"Him?" She laughed. "The day Barnabas becomes a dark reaper is the day that I'll kiss his amulet."

Silently we watched the kids pouring out of the school, each seeming to know exactly where they were going. Whether she knew it or not, Nakita's own views of the world were changing. When we had first met, she had been a typical dark reaper, ready to scythe people at a moment's notice to save their souls. To her, the body wasn't important. *Life* wasn't important. The soul was. It had taken me ages to get a grasp of that. Dark for heaven's fate, unseen; light for human's choice to glean.

Technically speaking, it was the light reapers who were the bad guys in heaven's sight, having been kicked out and banding together to protect those the dark reapers targeted. They saved lives at the expense of the soul. So who was doing the most good? I didn't know anymore.

Nakita was silent beside me, scanning faces. I wasn't sure if Tammy was going to be picked up by her mother, or if she was going to ride the bus home. "Maybe trying to find her at the school isn't such a good idea," I said. "Maybe we need to get closer," I added when Nakita said nothing.

"Why don't you try to use the time lines to find her?" she finally said. "Kairos always showed me the mark's aura in the time lines so I could recognize him or her by that."

I winced. "Tammy's aura, huh?" I offered. "That's great. Except I can't see auras."

"I can," Nakita said. "Kairos would show me the time line where he flashed, and the aura that mixed with his was the one we were looking for. We can do this, Madison." Her brow furrowed. "We can find her before Barnabas does, I bet."

A knot of tension eased in me, and I smiled. Barnabas. The rivalry was that bad, even now. "Worth a try," I said cheerfully, then turned my back on the school and sat down. The bars of the fence pushed into my back, and the grass tickled my ankles. Dappled sun made a cool wash of light on me. Taking a breath I didn't need other than to speak with, I exhaled, trying to settle myself using the technique that Barnabas had taught me. My hand crept up, and I grasped the stone that was at the center of my amulet. The silver wires cradling it were warm, and I closed my eyes. It was my amulet that let me see the time lines, and if I could use it to see auras, it would be a very good sign that I was becoming better at this.

Finding the time lines was easy, and with hardly any effort, I found the bright glow of the present, shifting off into infinity. Now all I had to do was find Tammy on it.

Everyone's life had a different color or aura. I couldn't see auras, but Barnabas had gone over them countless times as we sat on my roof and waited for the sun to rise. For most people the color was a reflection of their age and state of mind and could change with the seasons, but for reapers, it was a reflection of what side of the fate or free-will fence they were on. Light reapers tended to be a dark red in color, and dark reapers, violet, and those in the middle a neutral, greenish yellow. When I'd first met Barnabas, his amulet had been a respectable dark red. Now, though, it was clearly moving up the spectrum, showing more certainly than actions that he was starting to doubt his own beliefs. Doubt in an angel was a scary, unexpected thing, like finding out rocks were really made of water.

My original aura had been blue, or so Barnabas had once told me. Now it was violet, so dark it was basically black thanks to my timekeeper amulet. It was easy to find my aura in the bright time line, looking almost like a sinkhole. Beside me was Nakita's cheerful violet glow, her thoughts weaving among mine. Barnabas was absent, but if I looked down the fabric of time into the past, I could see where he had been with us. Josh, too. As I settled myself, Josh's aura jumped from somewhere else, joining mine and Nakita's. He was back from the mausoleum, and I didn't need to open my eyes to know it.

"Is she flashing forward again?" I heard him whisper.

"No," Nakita said softly. "She's searching the time lines for the mark's, uh, Tammy's aura."

"Really?" Josh said, and I heard him drop his gym bag. "What color is my aura?"

"Blue," she said tersely. "Shhh."

As soon as she said it, my entire thinking realigned. Given a name, the resonance I was seeing from Josh suddenly made sense. Blue. Josh's resonance was blue. I could see it in my mind so much clearer. Feeling more confident, I left the bright glow of Josh and Nakita to scan back a few hours earlier to the tangle of lines where I flashed forward at the track meet. I could feel Nakita's presence beside me, and together we looked to where my past twined with another, the weight of it seeming to make a dip in the fabric. The aura with mine was a sort of sick greenish color with a flash of orange at its center. Beside it was a bluish yellow one, slightly smaller. Her brother?

It had to be, and I eagerly opened my eyes. Josh was staring at me, having crouched to put us eye to eye, and I grinned right back at him. I couldn't decide, but there might have been a soft blue glow around him until the sun washed it out. Maybe I had a chance after all if I was really able to see auras.

"Was that her?" Nakita asked impatiently. "The greenish orange one?"

"You saw?" I said, relieved, and she nodded, smirking almost, as I let go of my amulet and the last visage of the time line vanished from my thoughts.

"Tammy has issues," she said, suddenly a lot more interested in the kids filing into buses or getting into cars. "But most seventeen-year-olds do."

Seventeen, same as me, or would be if I was alive. Josh stood, extending a hand to help me up. I took it, feeling a tingle between us. The glow about him seemed to strengthen, and I could see a red striation running through it, hovering even closer to his skin. It looked like it was fading, though, like a bruise. His near-death experience, maybe?

Nakita was holding the bars of the fence, her head gently resting between them as if she was in jail. I felt like I was one of the dead, spying on the living. Okay, technically I was, but being behind the graveyard fence only strengthened the emotion. Nakita's eyes closed, and she breathed deeply. "There's, like, twenty people the right age that have auras like that," she said. "Let's get closer."

Red purse tucked under her arm, she headed for the impressive gate, her sandals silent on the mown lawn. I brushed my jeans, glancing at Josh's school pants and shirt. He was going to be hot, but it was better than his running shorts and tank top. "If it helps, Tammy's brother has a bluish yellow aura," I said loudly.

"I saw that." Nakita turned to show me a worrisome smile. Predatory. Eager. Her fingers were on her amulet, the origin of her power and the source of her scythe.

Beside me, Josh hesitated. "She's not going to kill her, right?"

I shook my head, feeling he was right to ask. I picked up the pace to catch up with her. "Nakita?" I asked warily.

Nakita stopped, her hand on the gate and her eyes on the kids. There were fewer standing around outside now, and the first of the buses was leaving.

"I won't allow Ron to put a guardian angel on her," she said tightly. "You'd just better get Barnabas to do his part. But I'm telling you this isn't going to work. Marks never listen."

"Ace did." I was arguing with a brick wall, but even brick walls could be broken down. "Okay," I admitted as she tilted her head and raised her eyebrows questioningly at me. "So Ace is fated to live a short, violent life, but his soul isn't meaningless anymore and he gets people to think," I protested. "And what about Shoe? Now that he isn't taking the blame for trashing the hospital's system, he can help prevent that computer terrorist attack in the future. You can't tell me that's a bad thing."

"Life is transitory," she muttered, a whisper of doubt in her voice. "Only the soul matters." Checking to see that she had her precious camera, she lifted her head and started for the chipped curb. Josh laughed, and we bumped shoulders as he took my hand and we followed. Like magic, I felt as if the sun was warmer, the air fresher, and my step lighter. His hand in mine was cool, and he gave me a little squeeze, cementing our connection. Josh put up with a lot from me, and I was grateful he was here.

Short, violent life or not, I was proud of our success with Ace. Not only had we saved his soul and life, but we managed to keep his best friend, Shoe, out of the crapper, too.

It had been really hard, though, and our success was as much due to Shoe working to save his own skin as me, Barnabas, and Nakita trying to save it as well. Together Josh and I stepped up beside Nakita at the curb, squinting into the sun at the unfamiliar school. "I know that everyone thinks that Ace was a fluke," I said softly as Josh's hand slipped away with a last squeeze. "That's why we have to do it again."

Tucking her purse under her arm, Nakita shrugged. Clearly she didn't believe it was possible, but as far as I was concerned, this scything was already going better than the last. Nakita had agreed to not kill Tammy unless she was sure she couldn't be helped, and we knew where Tammy lived. We were halfway there.

"Is that them?" Nakita said suddenly, and I followed her pointing finger to a blonde girl standing impatiently with one foot on the steps of a bus, the other on the sidewalk. She was yelling at a cluster of boys still on the school steps, their heads together over a handheld game. "She's got a greenish aura with that orange center."

"Hold your horses!" a dark-haired boy yelled back, making an ugly face at her. "I've got to get to a portal, or I'm going to lose my place!"

"You're going to lose your ride home, you idiot!" she yelled back. "Mom is going to be ticked if she has to leave work to pick you up again, Johnny!"

The memory of my heart gave a pound and vanished. Johnny. That was Tammy's brother's name.

The girl turned in a huff and stomped up the stairs. In the line of buses, the second one revved its engine and left. Two more to go until Tammy's could leave.

"Your sister is a witch," I heard one of the boys say to Johnny, but Johnny was too engrossed in his game to comment.

"That's them," I said, suddenly worried. Now what?

Josh fidgeted as the next bus left. "Are we getting on?"

My lips pressed. Nakita could only carry one person in flight, and I didn't want to separate.

"Guys . . . the bus is leaving!" Josh said, motioning for us to run for it.

"Johnny!" the girl shouted out her window. "Get on the bus!"

A surge of excitement raced through me. "Let's go," I said, and we all broke into a jog. The bus was revving its engine. We slipped on right after Johnny, stomping up the stairs, Nakita first, then me, and lastly, Josh.

"Hey," the driver said, clearly not recognizing us, then he blinked. I could feel my amulet warming, and guessed that Nakita was doing something. The driver's gaze suddenly went unfocused, and I scrambled past him and into the aisle when he reached to pull the door shut. Josh barely made it.

I blew my breath out in relief. Thanks to Nakita, the driver either didn't see us, or didn't care. The kids, though, knew we didn't belong, and about fifteen pairs of eyes stared at us as we made our way down the aisle. Nervous, I worked my way to the back where Tammy sat with two girls, one with her, and one behind them, leaning over the back of their bench.

My unease grew as several pairs of eyes took in my purple-tinted hair, and someone snorted at my yellow shoes. Hand going to my amulet, I touched on the divine long enough to bend light around it, hiding the stone. I could still feel its original shape, but as far as anyone knew, it was just a silver chain.

I jumped when Josh touched my hand, and he grinned for having surprised me. Leaning forward, his breath tickling my neck and sending a shiver through me, he whispered, "I'm going to sit behind Johnny. See if I can learn anything."

"Okay," I whispered back, and he flopped into an empty seat, closing his eyes to look bored. His foot, though, was jiggling. He was enjoying this, and that made me feel good. Being the dark timekeeper's girlfriend was hard. It ought to have a few perks.

"There," I said to Nakita, pointing out the empty seat in front of Tammy.

Nakita sat stiffly, her nose wrinkled as if she smelled something bad. I agreed with her. I hadn't ridden the bus since I'd gotten my car a year ago. 'Course my car was still in Florida with my mom, but I'd rather ride my bike in the rain for five miles than take the bus now. I gingerly leaned back, my feet spread wide for balance as I fell into the half-aware stupor that the bus had always engendered in me. Slowly Nakita's posture eased as she took in my slouch and the barely contained havoc of the rest of the bus. It was noisy. I'd forgotten that part. Oh, joy.

The bus lurched, and I propped myself straight as we hit the main road. Slowly the noise evened out and the roaring of the diesel became a background hum. Okay, I'd found Tammy. Now the question was, how could I convince her to stay home tonight so her apartment wouldn't catch on fire, Johnny wouldn't die, and she wouldn't lose faith in herself and the world? It wasn't like I could turn around in the seat and tell her to make a better decision or her brother was going to go to the big arcade in the sky.

"Oh, it's to die for!" a loud voice said, too bold to be comfortable on my ears. "I saw it last night. His pants are so tight you could bounce a peanut butter cup off them, and I swear, his shirt had a new button undone in every scene."

"Good God, Jennifer," Tammy said. "What is it with you comparing boys to food?"

"So what?" the loud voice protested. "I'm going to see it again tonight. With Chris. You want to come? We can invite Dan and double date."

"I've got homework," a new voice said from right behind me, sort of a soft, quiet voice that sounded like it belonged to someone who had been beaten down one too many times by her friends. I knew that voice. It had never been mine, but I knew it.

"Homework," Jennifer snorted. "I knew you wouldn't come. I was talking to Tammy."

Beside me, Nakita started fiddling with her amulet. I glared at her, not wanting her to draw her sword. Barnabas would have a fit.

"Come on, Tammy," Jennifer coaxed. "You like Dan, right? Now's your chance to find out how good he can kiss."

"Uh . . . my mom . . ." Tammy started, and Jennifer laughed.

"Ple-e-e-ease!" she moaned. "There is no way your mom will find out. She's working."

"Yeah, but it's not like I can sneak out with Johnny around. The little brat will tattle on me."

"So wait until he's asleep. We're going to the late show, anyway."

The image of a burning building drifted before my eyes, and again, the terror of Tammy seeing the quietly flashing ambulance with its small, covered stretcher filled me. I turned my head just enough so I could see Jennifer leaning over the back of Tammy's seat, her arms dangling. Her expression was mocking, and I recognized that pissed look Tammy was now wearing. I'd been goaded by people I thought were my friends, too. She was going to do it, not because she wanted to sit in a dark theater with Dan, but because she didn't want Jennifer to think she was chicken.

"Look," Jennifer said, gum snapping, "wait for your mom to call at nine, like she *always* does, and then come out when bug boy is asleep. Easy peasy. You'll be home by twelve thirty."

The girl who had begged off with homework had her lips pressed, silently telling Tammy to say no. Jennifer saw it and pulled back a little. "You're chicken," she said derisively.

I sighed, knowing what was going to happen next.

"Am not!"

I held the edge of the seat as we took a corner, looking away when Jennifer's eyes met mine for a second. "Then I'll see you at ten thirty," the girl said, and I could feel her eyes on me still.

"Fine," Tammy said, and the memory of her terror hit me again.

"You can't!" I exclaimed, turning in the seat.

The three girls and Nakita stared at me, Nakita in wonder, Jennifer in anger, and Tammy and her last friend in bewilderment.

"Who asked you, you freak?" Jennifer said loudly.

My face warmed, but it wasn't like I could just turn back around. "I . . . uh," I stammered.

"Madison is not a freak," Nakita said hotly. "She's trying to save Tammy's soul."

My eyes shut, and I cringed. When they opened, Tammy's eyes were wide, and the girl with her looked afraid. Jennifer started to laugh. I was mortified. God, did Nakita even have a clue how lame that sounded? Even if it was true?

"What the hell?" Jennifer said. "Are you some kind of Bible school reject?"

My temper got the better of me, and I squinted at her. "Honey, the stuff I've done and gotten away with would put your daydreams to shame," I said, anger shoving my embarrassment to the back of my mind to deal with later. "So listen to me when I tell you sneaking out isn't worth it."

The sound of the fire roaring was echoed in the bus's engine, and I stifled a shiver as I looked at Tammy. Seeing her new resolve, I realized that speaking out had done more bad than good. She wanted freedom. She wanted to make her own decisions. But she clearly thought that making her own decisions meant doing the opposite of what her parents said was good for her. I'd call her a fool, but I'd been the same way myself. Until I had died trying to make a point that I was *no one's* little girl.

They were still staring at me. Maybe I should try a different tack.

"Look, all I'm saying is that stuff goes wrong sometimes," I said. "What if your little brother gets hurt? A burglar could break in, or the building could catch on fire. He'd be all alone."

Jennifer flopped back into her seat. "In this town? You gotta be kidding me. Nothing happens here. Mind your own business."

Nakita reached for her amulet, and I gently kicked her ankle. Her gaze shot to mine, her eyes seeming to say, "I told you so."

I was hot with anger. I don't know how, because I was

dead and didn't really have a body, but I was definitely warm. Disconcerted, I turned around, very aware of them still staring at me.

I couldn't bring myself to look at Nakita. I didn't want her to be right. There was no way that I was going to spend the next thousand years sending out assassin angels to end lives in order to save souls. I stood when the bus lurched to a halt.

Nakita rose with me. "We're getting off? What about . . . her?"

My eyes were fixed on the front as three kids filed off. "Tammy will be fine until tonight. We need to leave before I shove my amulet down Jennifer's throat." I looked back at Nakita, who still hadn't gotten into the aisle. "Come on. We know where she lives. Or Barnabas does."

Nodding, Nakita followed me to the front. "We're leaving?" Josh said as I touched his shoulder, but he immediately picked up his gym bag and stood.

From the back of the bus, Jennifer said in a mocking falsetto, "Going home to play tea party with your dolls?"

Josh winced at my pressed lips and warm cheeks. "Time to leave. Gotcha."

"Before Madison learns how to use her amulet and scythes the wrong girl," Nakita said, clearly amused.

"I can't believe I just blurted it out like that," I berated myself. "I am such an idiot."

"Didn't go well, huh?" Josh asked as he filed out behind

Nakita, and we all got off the bus.

"That's one way to put it," I said, hands on my hips and staring at the bus from the sidewalk. Tammy was watching me, and Jennifer was making angelic faces looking heavenward. I hated that they were laughing at me, especially with Josh watching.

Nakita and Josh were beside me, and I held my breath as the bus drove away. The three kids who got off with us gave us a long look before heading down the sidewalk.

"Madison?" Josh asked, and I exhaled.

"It's okay," I said, trying to get rid of my anger. I hadn't handled it well, but it was only my second scything. "We know who she is, and what she's doing tonight. That's more than we did ten minutes ago." I glanced at my watch, surprised to find out it had only been just that long. "Barnabas is probably a few houses up," I said as I put my hands in my jeans pockets and started to follow the bus's route. "You want to just walk it?"

Josh immediately shouldered his bag and fell into step beside me. Nakita, though, lingered behind, head down, arms crossed over her middle—thinking.

THREE

The loud bang of the Laundromat's door hitting the wall brought Barnabas's eyes up from where he sat with an untouched vendor-dispensed coffee before him. I watched the woman who just left drag her bratty kid to the busy street, not even using the cross-walk to dart over the six lanes to reach the apartment complex on the other side. The building was the same one from my flash forward—minus the fire trucks. The air-conditioning was on in here, but it was humid from the dryers, and it smelled like bad coffee and fabric softener. The place was empty now, apart from us, and Josh leaned over to open the dryer that someone had left going. The heat billowed out to warm my feet, and slowly the noise died to nothing.

Josh slid from the dryer, sighing as he went to stand before the concession machine. He jiggled the change in his pocket before exchanging it for a double-stuffed, massive cookie the size of a plate. I looked at it enviously as he brought it back and slumped into the couch beside me. Nakita was in the chair next to Barnabas, and I propped my feet up on the table.

"You found the place okay?" I asked Barnabas as Josh took a huge bite, white cream squishing out the back.

Barnabas nodded, running a hand over his loose curls as his gaze went out the window to the apartment building. "How about you? Did you find Tammy?"

Nakita rolled her eyes and set her purse on the table. "She blew it."

My brow furrowed, and Barnabas's eyes widened. "She's dead?"

"She is not dead!" I said, then lowered my voice when an attendant poked his head in before vanishing into a back room. A sitcom laugh track rose faintly, and I leaned toward Barnabas. "I know who she is. Blonde. Bossy—"

"And thinks Madison is a wacko," Nakita said as she snapped open her purse and brought her camera out. Focusing on the rows of silent washers, lids up, she added, "You just *had* to blurt it out."

"Hey. I'm not the one telling her I'm trying to save her soul," I said, and Barnabas exhaled loudly.

Totally unperturbed, Nakita looked at the back of her camera and the digital screen. "Stay home or you'll ruin your life was the first thing out of her mouth. We had to get off the bus." Glancing at Barnabas, she added, "Did you see Tammy get off?"

Barnabas pulled himself out of his slouch. "Could have. I saw a girl the right age get off the bus with a boy. She looked scared."

I nodded. "That was probably her. Jeans, pink shirt. Blonde?"

"Yup, she lives on the third floor, corner apartment." Barnabas sipped his machine-made drink, grimaced, and set it down. "Sweet seraphs, this is bad. So what happened on the bus?"

My focus blurred as I thought back to it. Maybe I hadn't screwed things up too badly. "Other than she and her friends thinking I was a freak of a Goody Two-shoes? I don't know. If she looked scared, maybe she'll stay home tonight instead of going to the movies to swap spit with David."

"It was Dan," Nakita said, and I rolled my eyes.

"Dan then. But if her brother doesn't die, she won't run away, right? Problem solved."

Nakita, though, didn't look convinced as she exchanged a worried look with Barnabas. "What?" I asked, thinking they knew something I didn't.

Josh turned his cookie around to lick the cream squishing out. He looked happy and content, and I shifted my leg until our knees touched. He smiled as he looked up, making me glad he was here with me. "Don't you ever stop eating?" Nakita asked him.

"No." Josh turned to look at the vending machine. "You

chipped your nail polish."

Nakita gasped, immediately checking her fingernails, then bending first one sandal up to check her toes, then the other. "I did not!" she exclaimed indignantly.

Barnabas was smiling, and Josh held the last of his cookie up. "Madison, you want one?"

I shook my head, and Nakita glared at him. "She doesn't eat, mortal."

"It's still polite to ask," Josh said, chewing, and if I was able to blush, I would have. "Barnabas, did they tell you yet that Madison identified Tammy by her aura?"

A jolt of excitement raced through me, and I sat up, having forgotten my success there. "No," Barnabas said, looking as happy as I suddenly felt. "Madison, that's fantastic! How long have you been able to see auras?"

"I can't," I said, though I was starting to wonder.

Nakita, too, was smiling again. "She looked back through at the time line to where she flashed so I could see Tammy's aura resonance. She's a fish."

"Green with an orange center," Barnabas said cryptically. "She's got issues."

"Fish?" I asked, wondering if it was some kind of code.

"My aura is blue," Josh said.

Barnabas looked askance at him. "I know," he said, then turned to me. "So you talked to her. You scared her. You think it was enough?"

I shrugged, glancing at Josh's cookie. "I don't know. It's not like I zap back home when reality realigns itself. I want to talk to her again."

"There's a good idea."

Ignoring Barnabas, I licked my lips, wishing I was hungry. "That looks good, Josh."

Josh beamed as he stood up. "I'll get you one."

"She doesn't eat . . . Josh," Nakita said dryly, then took a picture of everyone's feet and the crumbs he had made.

I shook my head, and Josh sat back down. "Thanks, anyway," I said softly. "I'll be glad when I learn how to look between the now and the next and find my body. I'm tired of not being hungry."

Nakita froze, and I looked up to find her staring at me. Her eyes blinked, and in a sudden motion, she shoved her camera into her purse. "I'll be outside watching the apartment," she said, then walked quickly to the door, her back stiff and her pace stilted. The door hit the wall, making a bigger dent, and then she was outside, standing with her arms crossed and her head down in the fading sun.

Bewildered, I looked from Josh, his mouth full and chewing slowly, to Barnabas's resigned expression. "What did I say?" I asked.

Josh shrugged, but Barnabas winced. "She's worried that once you get your body back that you'll dissociate from your amulet and leave her. So am I."

Worried, I looked out the plate-glass windows.

"Those black wings you put in her left some of your memories in her. She knows you better than anyone on heaven or earth, and she's afraid. I'll be okay, but Nakita . . . You taught her what it's like to fear death, and she thinks that once you're gone no one will understand her and people will think she's more of a square peg than they already do."

Oh, God. How do I get into these messes?

Josh jumped when his phone vibrated. Excusing himself, he went to answer it and give us some privacy at the same time. My gaze dropped, and I ran my fingernail along a groove in the table. Looking up, I gathered my determination. "I don't want to give up being the dark timekeeper," I said. "But if I can't make this work—if I can't convince the seraphs that the early scythings are unnecessary to save a person's soul before it goes bad, then I'm not going to stay around to send reapers to kill people who are too scared, or frightened, or *just plain stupid* to find joy in life."

Barnabas looked out the window, his hat pulled low over his eyes. "You wanted to know what was bothering her. That's it."

He was being unusually callous, and I frowned. "You don't think I'd rather stay here with you?" I almost growled, crumpling up Josh's cookie wrapper. "I'm trying to make this work!"

"So is she." Barnabas leaned forward. "She hasn't been on earth as long as I have. She doesn't understand about human choice and the fragility of your dreams and the strength that lies in your hopes and faith. Angels see everything in black and white, and the earth was made to be colorful. Think about what you're asking her to do. She is all about the soul, Madison. Life is secondary to her. Life is transient, and you're asking her to risk someone's soul for an extension of something that to her is a blink of an eye."

"But all we have is that blink," I said miserably.

Barnabas leaned back and glanced at Josh, talking with someone on the phone. "I know. It's one of the reasons I left heaven. I think that Nakita is starting to understand. She's come a long way."

My throat was tight, and I watched Josh close his phone, looking as depressed as I felt. "So have you, Barnabas," I said softly.

Frowning, Barnabas looked away. I knew he wasn't happy about leaving his light-reaper status. My special talent seemed to be screwing up everyone's life. Sighing, I watched Nakita standing in the lowering sun looking perfect and worried. She wasn't a fallen angel like Barnabas, but one in good standing. So far. But I'd scarred her, changed her forever when I had accidentally put two black wings inside her. They had been eating me alive when I'd lost contact with my amulet and had fallen through her like a ghost. The black wings had latched on to her and started to eat her memories, much richer than mine. Eventually the seraphs had gotten them out, but the memories that the black wings had taken from me were forever a part of her. She now knew what it was like to fear, something that most angels have no concept of.

"I don't want to leave," I whispered.

Barnabas made a small noise. "Then we'd better make this work."

Josh shuffled up, his eyes darting from me to Barnabas. "I have to go," he said in disgust. "My mom found out I wasn't at The Low D with the guys and wants me home."

"Oh, no!" I exclaimed, guilt from making him lie for me rising up fast. "Josh, I'm so sorry. I didn't mean to get you in trouble."

He shrugged, head down as he zipped his gym bag shut. "I told her I took you to dinner instead, and she's not mad, but I gotta go put in an appearance. You'd better call your dad. She might have phoned him."

I hated this. Lying. It made more trouble than it solved, but what were my choices here? *Hey, Dad. I'm on the West Coast tonight, trying to stop a boy from dying in an apartment fire. Back after midnight! Love you!*

Throwing my head back, I looked at the stained ceiling. Someone had put graffiti up there, and I blinked. Barnabas silently stood and shook out his long duster like it was his wings. "I'll take you home," he offered to Josh.

"Puppy presents," I swore softly, standing as well. "Do you think you can come back?"

Josh hoisted his gym bag to his shoulder and brushed the

cookie crumbs from his shirt. "I don't know. I'll cover for you best I can, but if anyone asks, I left you at The Low D with a couple of girls."

I made a face. Yeah, that was likely. I only had one girlfriend, and she was out at the curb, afraid I was going to ditch her.

Josh glanced at his watch, still set for Illinois time. "It's almost six thirty at home." Frustrated, he dropped his hand and grimaced. "I might not be able to get away until after midnight, which will be ten here. Everything might be done by then."

"If we're lucky." I glanced at Barnabas, knowing that he wasn't going to sit and wait for Josh. He'd come right back. "Well, I'm going to have to put in an appearance tonight, too," I said, thinking of my curfew. At least it was the weekend. "Call me?"

Josh smiled at that, and my entire frame of mind changed when he edged around the table and took my hands and pulled gently, hesitantly. I leaned in as he did, and he gave me a kiss.

He smelled like soap, and his lips quirked in a soft smile when he pulled away. "Soon as I know what's up, I'll call," he said. "Maybe I can get away sooner."

"Okay." I felt soft and squishy, and I let his fingers slip from mine reluctantly. Outside, Nakita was frowning, but Barnabas patiently waited.

Shifting his gym bag higher, Josh leaned toward me again, and after one last kiss, he rocked back, smiling.

"Come on, Buck Rogers," Barnabas said as he motioned to the door. "Let's go."

Giving me a last look, Josh headed for the parking lot. "Who's Buck Rogers?" he asked as the door opened, Barnabas catching it before it hit the wall.

I slowly sank back down in my chair, still feeling the warmth of those two kisses. Such a small thing, but not really. My smile fading, I watched Barnabas talk to Nakita. The dark reaper glanced at me, then away. I couldn't help but wonder what he'd said to her as he started walking away with Josh.

Stretching out my leg, I shoved the dryer door shut with my foot, then stood to push the button to get it started again. The soft hum and sliding *schlummp, schlummp, schlummp* of someone's jeans slowly filled the steamy room. Head down, I leaned over the adjacent dryer, wondering if Nakita would come in or continue to boycott me. I wished that Josh could have stayed, but I'd be lying if I didn't admit that having him at home to help me if I needed it was a comfort. Being two time zones from home made it hard to cover one's tracks. Even if one was a timekeeper.

The faint humming in my legs grew stronger. Realizing it wasn't coming from the adjacent dryer, I pulled my head up. The world had gone blue. Like I was in a gigantic fishbowl in reverse, the parking lot beyond the huge plate-glass windows was a sunny, inky blue, but even as I stared, the fluorescent lights in the Laundromat began dripping an insidious indigo. I was going to flash.

We've done it! I thought joyfully, eyes alight as I looked for

Nakita, her back to me as she watched Barnabas and Josh leave. Why else would I flash forward unless Tammy had indeed changed her fate?!

My hand rose to grip my amulet, shocked to find it more than warm. It was hot! "Nakita!" I shouted, and she turned. Her eyes widened at something she saw in me, and I heard her mental shout to Barnabas echo as it hit the top of the atmosphere and bounced back.

And then the inky black poured from the ceiling lights. It billowed up around my knees, and, like a deadly gas, it hit me hard. My knees gave way, and I fell, one hand still holding the top of the dryer. The heat of it seemed to burn my fingers, and I couldn't see. The blue stuff had gotten in my eyes and they were tearing. Suddenly I realized I wasn't crumpled on the floor of the Laundromat with my fingertips warm on the dryer.

I was in Tammy, her fingers burning, and she was terrified.

Choking, hot air burned in my mouth, and my lungs ached. I couldn't breathe. "Johnny!" I screamed, then hunched over, coughing. I fell, arms outstretched. It was dark, and I gasped when my cheek hit the carpet. The air down here was a blessed few degrees cooler, and I cried as I pulled it into my damaged lungs. I was dying. I had died before, and I knew the feeling though Tammy didn't—the same blackness edging my vision, and the same lack of pain filled my arms and legs.

No! I thought, confused. I had changed things! We had talked to Tammy! This couldn't be the future, could it? Was there going to be a happy ending to this? There had to be. But the flash forward said otherwise, and by the lack of any blue haze, it looked like it was going to be tonight, not tomorrow. Damn it, I'd made things worse, not better.

"Johnny!" I cried again, crawling to his door. I found it, reaching up to turn the knob and push the door open. A wave of sound rushed out over my head, and I cowered in the sudden heat.

"Tammy!" I heard him call, and I crawled forward, scared out of my mind. I could smell things burning, and my mind walled the horror away. Everything. Everything was on fire.

And then I found him.

He was blind with terror, but at my touch, he grasped me, and we clung together as the ceiling above us turned into a beautiful, rolling orange and red. It was mesmerizing, even as my eyelashes singed and my nose burned inside.

"Tammy, I'm scared," Johnny whispered, coughing, and I held him. It was too late. We couldn't get out. Crying, I rocked him, our backs to the wall beside his bed.

"I'm here," I whispered, Tammy's last breath rasping as our twined thoughts were voiced by her alone. "You're not alone. I've got you."

And then we looked up as a roaring sound of heat sucked a new breath of air into the room an instant before the ceiling gave way. Everything flashed red—

I jumped, feeling as if someone had slapped me. Terrified, my eyes sprang open.

"Barnabas!" I cried. He was crouched before me, his eyes intent. It was over. But what had happened? The memory of my heart was thudding after having been inside Tammy, and slowly it beat one last time and stopped. Her terror took longer to leave me, and I sat there clutching my cooling amulet as Nakita and Josh clustered around me in concern.

"You came back," I said, thinking it sounded lame, and Barnabas shifted a few inches away. Standing, he extended his hand and pulled me, wobbling, to my feet.

The humid air of the Laundromat seemed cool. Tears were dribbling from me. I slowly leaned back against the thumping dryer, my arms wrapped around myself as I started to shake, the tears steadily slipping from me. It was awful. So awful.

"What happened?" Josh asked, but I couldn't talk. Not yet. They had died. Both of them. This was so unfair. Johnny and Tammy had died with grace, supporting each other in a way that was beautiful and showed the best of a human soul, but they had died. It wasn't what I had wanted. Her soul might be saved, but it was the end of her life that had bought its purity.

"Something changed?" Nakita asked, but by her tone of voice, she knew it wasn't good.

I looked past them at the empty Laundromat as if it was a dream and would flake into nothing and return me to that hell of existence, the fear, the hopelessness, the love for her brother giving Tammy something to believe in. "They both die," I whispered.

"In a state of grace," Barnabas finished for me, his brow furrowed.

Josh rocked back, looking worried. I would never tell him of the horror I'd just lived through. "I didn't save Tammy's or Johnny's life," I said. "All I did was make it so a reaper didn't have to come out here and scythe her early. God, this sucks!" Depressed, I closed my eyes and wiped a tear away. I couldn't do this. It was too much. It hurt too much when things went wrong.

"We have to do something," Nakita said, and my eyes opened. She was standing over the table, her lips pressed in determination. "Now," she said firmly. "We have to go now."

"But her soul is safe," I said, wanting to do just that but surprised that Nakita did, too. "Why do you care?"

Her hand on the door, Nakita paused, looking at me to make me shiver. "Her soul may be safe, but mine is troubled."

FOUR

The memory of fire trucks that existed only in the future seemed to haze over my sight as I looked across the busy road to the three-story apartment complex. Having watched—no, lived— Tammy and Johnny dying in a fire had more than shaken me. It had rocked me to my core. I'd thought that I'd made a difference, but all I'd done was make things worse. Josh, at least, got home safely. He'd been gone only five minutes, and I missed him already. I worried that he was going to drift away, looking for someone who wasn't being yanked across the continent to save someone she didn't even know, someone who didn't have to lie to her dad all the time, someone who had friends other than angels—and someone who could eat a friggin' bowl of popcorn with him. Why couldn't I just be normal?

I sniffed, jumping when Nakita handed me a tissue from

her purse. "Thanks," I said as I rubbed the soft paper under my nose and wadded it up in a tight ball. God, I was going to throw up, I knew it.

"I'm sorry, Madison," she said as she stood awkwardly next to me while we waited for traffic to clear enough to cross.

"Me too," I said, glancing back when Barnabas dropped from the sky, a soft thump of air giving him away. His expression was cross, and his wings immediately vanished, leaving him a slightly surly, broody teenager in dark pants, a faded band tee, and a black duster totally at odds with the hot weather. He shoved his hands in his pockets and joined us at the curb, just back from his quick trip to take Josh home. Josh said he was going to cover for me, but I was likely still going to have to make an appearance for my dad before too long.

I turned back, waiting for a light to change about half a mile up the road. Barnabas was upset, looking positively angry as he scowled at Nakita, something clearly on his mind. I'd be concerned, but disappointment clung to me like a second shadow, made worse by the darkening sky. Heat stored in the asphalt rose, and I brushed the hair from my eyes as I scanned the skies for black wings that wouldn't be coming. No, I'd fixed everything up just jim dandy. Thanks to me, Tammy would die without reaper intervention. The seraphs were probably tickled three shades of happiness. I was truly the dark timekeeper, able to convince people to kill themselves after a few minutes' conversation.

"You do not have a soul," Barnabas muttered to Nakita out of the blue, shocking me. "Only creatures of the earth have souls."

Souls? I wondered, my thoughts going back to Nakita's last words before he had left, and I turned to see her standing with her lips pressed and her grip tight on her red purse.

"I do, too," she said defiantly, but she looked frightened as well. "I fear," she said as if finding strength in it for the first time. "I'm creative. I think I could love. I say that means I have a soul. It might not be perfect, like Madison's, but I've got one. And it might be in danger if I just let Tammy die."

Bemused, I looked at them both, Nakita flustered and looking like she'd done something wrong, and Barnabas, angry and surly. "You guys don't have souls?" I asked, and Barnabas dropped his gaze to his faded sneakers.

"Angels don't," he said bitterly, almost jealously. "Even ones kicked out of heaven."

A semi clattered past, and I held my hair to my head. "Who says?"

"*I* have a soul," Nakita said firmly, but her expression was haunted. "I have a piece of Madison's."

Mine? How could she have a part of my soul?

"I . . . don't think I can give it back to you," Nakita said. "I'm sorry." She was pleading, looking both frightened and desperate, her blue eyes pinched in concern. "It's just a little sliver from yours, it got stuck in me with the black wings. I'll ask the seraphs to try to take it from me if you want it back. It might make things easier. I don't think we're supposed to have one—"

"No!" I said immediately, and Barnabas's eyes squinted. "No," I said softer. "You keep it. Are you sure? I mean, I don't feel like I'm missing anything."

Nakita's smile was blissful, as if a great guilt had been lifted from her. "I feel it," she said firmly. "I knew it was there ever since the black wings, but I didn't know what it was because sometimes it makes me hurt inside, but even then it feels good." Shyly, she looked up at me from lowered eyes. "Thank you."

I touched her arm so she'd realize I knew what it meant to her. "You're welcome." She had a part of my soul? Jeez, just how much had I ruined her existence?

"You do not have part of Madison's soul," Barnabas said disdainfully.

"I do!" Nakita's anger flared. "You need to shut up, you filthy light reaper! You don't have one, so you don't know anything about it!"

"Nakita," I admonished, but it almost looked like Barnabas appreciated the insult—even if it was technically inaccurate. His eyes were on the traffic, and I followed his gaze to guess that it was clear enough to cross with two angels with me. "Let's go," I said. "Nakita, I'm glad you have a part of my soul. It's the least I can do for having put black wings inside you. Keep it. Make it yours."

My feet hit the pavement, and the heat rose up in a wave. I

could hear them following, going slow, then fast as cars came and went around us. Barnabas hustled to catch up, and as we reached the curb, he whispered, "Do you think she really has part of your soul?"

I shrugged. "If she says so. I don't feel like I'm missing anything."

Nakita strolled past us, intent on reaching the apartment building. She looked breezy and bright, clearly relieved that the question of her soul had been settled. "Tammy is on the third floor. I can sense her resonance."

Barnabas and I found the sidewalk together. He looked angry. "Barnabas," I started, and he interrupted me.

"I'm fine," he said brusquely.

"Who's to say you don't have a soul?" I said. "Maybe that's why you got kicked out of heaven in the first place?"

His pace faltered, and he looked at me in wonder. Something in me ached to see him hurting inside this much. "I don't have a soul," he said, but there was a thread of doubt in it. "We weren't made to have one. We were made to serve, not delight in God's creations."

Serve? I thought, then filed that away to think about later. "Well, you did get kicked out because you loved someone, right?" I said, watching my shoes scuff the thick cracks as we slowly followed Nakita. It was the first time I dared to ask him about his past, and though he seemed uncomfortable, I wanted to know. "And you found value in life, not just someone's soul.

You can't value something you don't have, can you?"

"N-no," he stammered, but Nakita had already opened the front door and was waiting for us. The cool air flowed out, but that wasn't why I shivered. *Barnabas has a soul, doesn't he?*

I followed Nakita inside, seeing the faded carpet with the flat, black spots that had to be old gum. It smelled like dry dirt, and there was a thick layer of dust on the narrow sections of hardwood between the carpeted stairs and the wall. A bank of mail slots took up one wall with a scratched table under it. There were a couple of pieces of mail sitting there, and nothing else.

"Upstairs?" I offered, and Nakita started up, then me, and finally Barnabas, still probably thinking about his soul or the lack of one. Someone was playing music too loudly, and it rapidly grew as we ascended.

We rounded the second landing and started up the last stairway. The music was coming from the third floor. It thumped into me, the bass being joined by a guitar and an angry vocal the higher we went. My curiosity turned into a wince as I realized that the aggressive music was coming from the apartment that Nakita had stopped in front of. C3, corner apartment, top floor. It went without saying that Tammy's mom was probably not home.

Suddenly unsure, I wiped my hands on my jeans. I didn't have a clue what I could say that wouldn't sound crazy. I didn't *care* if I sounded crazy at this point. The memory of the two of them dying was too awful to risk becoming true.

"Well?" Nakita prompted.

"This is a bad plan," Barnabas said, but he leaned past me, ringing the bell and knocking on the varnished door.

Plan? Who said anything about a plan? I don't even have a plan! I thought in panic as a dog began to yap wildly, and the thin strip of light coming from under the door was eclipsed by frantic little paws. From behind the door came a kid's voice telling the dog to shut up, and then, with a burst of music, the door opened.

"Yeah?" Johnny said, hardly looking up from his handheld game as Seether's "Fake It" blasted. With one foot, he shoved the little yellow dog back. He was still dressed in his school clothes, and the polo shirt and black Dockers looked out of place in the untidy living room behind him with its dirty dishes on the coffee table. The adjoining dining room wasn't much better, the table covered in what looked like college textbooks. To the right was the open kitchen, just off the narrow entryway. I blanched at the memory of the room in flame, and my eyes went to the ceiling, recalling the beautiful, deadly curls of gold and black and the searing heat in my lungs as Johnny died in my arms.

Tonight? I wondered, scared. It had to be. The vision had been very clear.

"Is your sister here?" Barnabas finally said, since I was lost in the horror of the memory.

Still playing his game, Johnny dropped back. "Tammy!" he shouted over the music. "Your friends are here!" Head down, he walked to his room off to the left. From the kitchen, the phone began to ring. The dog, too, was still barking. Not knowing what to do, we all stood in the doorway.

"Come on in," Johnny said, walking backward and killing ninjas at the same time, and then louder called, "Tammy!" Without looking up, he edged into his room and shoved the door closed.

I looked at the two of them, and then the empty room. "Should we go in?"

Barnabas pushed forward. "I would," he said, positioning himself just over the threshold. "Otherwise as soon as she sees us, she's going to slam the door in our faces."

"Have some faith, Barnabas," I said as I followed Nakita in and stood with my feet just on the linoleum that marked the beginning of the kitchen.

"I have lots of faith," the fallen angel said as he crouched and coaxed the dog closer. "I have faith that this is a bad idea. She's not going to believe you. She's going to think we're nuts. She's going to call the police unless she has a record, and if she does, she'll run away."

I frowned, glancing at the front door. It didn't seem right to shut it.

Nakita shifted to stand even deeper in the kitchen, positioning herself so she could see the entire main room. "There's a lot of noise in here," she said, looking at the phone, still ringing.

Maybe a fried stereo would be what started the fire. I was starting to wonder how these two had survived even this long when from a back bedroom came a frustrated, "I said, would you get that, Johnny?"

The volume of the music suddenly halved. Three seconds later, the door across the living room from Johnny's was yanked open and Tammy strode out, her hair swinging as she stomped into the living room and started throwing couch pillows as she looked for the phone.

"Where's the friggin' phone?" she muttered, snatching it up. Her eyes were narrowed and she looked mad. Spinning, she jerked to a stop as she saw us all standing in the kitchen, Barnabas still crouched as he rubbed the ears of the little dog. The phone in her hand rang again, seeming to jerk her out of her surprise.

"Oh, no," she said, recognizing me. "Get out!" she shouted, waving her arm at me. "Johnny! You're not supposed to let anyone in!"

"It's for you!" came his hidden voice. "I'm not your stupid secretary."

Expression dark, she started for us, halting as she realized how vulnerable she was. Holding the phone like a weapon, she snapped, "Get out," before thumbing the phone line open.

"Hello?" she said, watching us stand there. "I'm sorry, Mr. Tambu. Johnny turned it up when I was in the bathroom. It's down now." She frowned. "I said I'm sorry!" she said, then hung up on him. Shaking, she faced us. "I told you to get out!" she said loudly, but she looked scared, making me wonder why she hadn't told her neighbor we were up here.

"Tammy, just listen," I said, thinking that leaving the door open might have helped. "We're not going to hurt you. You're in trouble."

"I'm in trouble?" Tammy pointed the phone at us. "I'm not the one breaking and entering! Get the hell out or I'm calling the police!"

But she hadn't yet, so I didn't think she would. From her room the music shifted to something darker, more dangerous.

Barnabas stood up from petting the dog, looking calm and casual, like the lead singer in a boy band. "It will take them forty minutes to get here," he said, his voice soothing, beautiful. "If you listen to us, we'll leave in three."

Tammy swallowed and Nakita rolled her eyes at the effect he had on her. "Who are you?" she asked him. "You weren't on the bus."

"Barnabas." He smiled, and I almost groaned as he charmed her. Good grief, he was better at this than Nakita and me put together, and yet he still harbored doubts we could make a difference.

Nakita edged forward. "We're trying to help. Your soul is safe, but not your life."

Tammy's expression immediately shifted back to mistrust.

"Nakita!" I all but hissed at her. "Will you shut up about souls! Everyone thinks we're nuts when you talk about souls like they're as common as TVs."

She looked at me innocently. "But they are."

"That doesn't mean we talk about them!" I said, exasperated.

Tammy was eyeing us between glances at the door, the phone still in her hand. "Did my mom send you? Is this her perverted way of checking up on me?" she asked. "God! It's like a police state around here. You can tell her to stay out of my life! I'm not a baby!"

Her mom? I wish. "Your mom doesn't know we're here," I said, thinking it would help.

Barnabas threw the dog's toy, and the little thing tore after it. "Is that Soap Scum?" he asked, and I stared until I realized he was talking about the music.

"Yeah," Tammy said, losing her aggressive stance again. "You've heard of them?"

He smiled. "I saw them in concert in Chicago, right before the drummer died from a heart attack."

Nakita snorted. "Did you mess up his scythe prevention, too?"

Barnabas frowned, taking the dog's toy as the animal jumped at his knees. "No. I was there for one of the kids in the audience."

"Scythe prevention?" Tammy whispered. She looked at the phone in her hand and took a step back. "What are you guys trying to be? Grim reapers?"

"No," Nakita said before I could tell her to shut up. "We're dark reapers." She hesitated, then added, "I think. Madison, if we're trying to save lives, then are we technically light?"

"No," I said, worried about Tammy's expression. This was going sour fast. There were too many people mucking it up, and I couldn't get to why I was here. "Tammy, two minutes," I said. "That's it. You listen for two minutes, and we'll leave. I know this looks weird, but we're trying to help. If you don't listen to me, you're going to die tonight. Johnny, too."

Her expression blanched, and Barnabas leaned toward me. "Uh, that might not have been the best thing to say," he whispered.

Tammy gestured violently. "Get out!" she shouted. "Get out, or I'm calling the cops!"

She was frantic, and I stumbled when Barnabas took my shoulder and drew me back.

"Tammy, there's a fire!" I said loudly, not caring if I sounded crazy or not. The horror had been too real. "I watched you both die. You need to leave tonight. Just go somewhere else! Anywhere!"

"And you think me talking about souls makes us sound crazy," Nakita said.

"Get out!"

Tammy was screaming, and Johnny had opened his door, staring at us with one eye through the crack.

"I told you this wouldn't work," Barnabas said, his grip on my elbow tightening as he pulled me back another step.

"Okay, okay!" I said, scrambling. We were backing up past the fridge, and I grabbed the little sticky note from it that had a grocery list on it. The little pencil tied to it swung, and I caught it. "I'm going to give you a number," I said, writing it down. "Call this guy, okay? His name is Shoe. He's in Iowa. I helped him last month. Well, I helped his buddy Ace, but Ace is in a mental institution right now, so you're going to have to talk to Shoe." *You can shut up anytime now, Madison.*

"You're just like friggin' Mary Poppins, huh?" Tammy said sarcastically, clearly feeling braver now that we were backing toward the door.

"Just call him," I said. "He was going to be accused of killing three people when his friend dumped a computer virus he made into a hospital system and screwed it up. We managed to fix that. We're trying to help, Tammy!"

She stood with her arms crossed, phone tucked against her. "You're crazy."

I bumped into Nakita, and the warmth of the hall soaked into me. "Just call him, okay? And here's my cell number. Call me when you want to talk."

"One way or another, she's not going to be alive when the sun comes up," Nakita said dryly, and I took a deep breath, feeling my heels scuff on the carpet in the hall.

"Call Shoe," I said, throwing the pad of paper to the floor

between us. "Find out I'm not crazy. Or don't call him, I don't care. Just don't be here tonight. You or Johnny. I know he's a pain, but take him with you when you go to the movies, or ice cream, or whatever. Just don't be here! You've got to believe me, Tammy! There's going to be a fire!"

She had come forward, more confident now that we were in the hall. Johnny was wide-eyed behind her, and the dog was wagging his tail, toy in his mouth. Tammy glared at us, but it was Johnny who picked up the piece of paper with the phone number. With a shove, she slammed the door shut in our faces. The thump echoed in the hallway. From inside, the music grew louder.

"That went well," Barnabas said glumly, his hands in his pockets.

FIVE

Closing my phone, I tucked it away, having texted *CUL8R, THX* to Josh after his message that he was on his way to bed but wanted to give it another thirty minutes before trying to sneak out. I glanced at Barnabas sitting next to me between the outside wall of the Laundromat and the Dumpster. If it was nine here, it was eleven at home. I had an hour before my curfew. I didn't know when the fire was going to start, but Tammy had been outside of the apartment in my first flash, so it was likely going to happen sometime between nine and midnight, local time. It'd be just my luck that the fire would start when I was convincing my dad I was going to bed.

Right now, Tammy and Johnny were out. Barnabas and I were watching to make sure it stayed that way.

Across the street, the apartment complex had come alive

with lights and the sound of too many TVs. From the Laundromat, we had watched the cop car, which Tammy had called, leave about an hour ago. It had taken them almost three hours to show up and forty minutes to leave, both cops laughing at Tammy's story as they got in their vehicle and drove away, which was really sad because three crazy people *had* been in her house uninvited, and they weren't taking her seriously. Tammy and Johnny had left right after the cops, Johnny whining as she dragged him down the sidewalk as the sun went down, looking scared as she got into her friend Jennifer's dented two-door. I should've felt relieved that she'd taken my advice and left, but the fear that they might come back had me tense and worried.

It was dark now, the lights from the cars between us and the apartment complex creating moving spots of clarity in an otherwise depressing night. Nakita was out doing a flyby of the area. My back was to the red bricks, and my knees were bent almost to my chin as I swung my amulet on its silver chain, idly concentrating on it to shift its form. It was a skill that Nakita had taught me.

I miss Josh. "Barnabas," I said softly, feeling alone though he sat right next to me. "You have a soul. How can you not?"

He was silent, watching as I played with the glittery black stone safely encased in its wrapping of wire. I focused on it, modulating the light bending around it until it looked like a little silver cross with a black stone in the center.

"You are the best of us," I said, looking at my amulet. I was pleased with the result, though it still felt like an oval, river-washed stone to my fingers. "Unflawed and beautiful. You have to have a soul."

"Angels weren't made for the earth," he said. "Only those of the earth have souls."

"Okay, but you abandoned heaven for earth," I said, not believing that God would be so cruel. But then again, look what he'd fated for me. "Maybe that means you really belonged here. That you've had a soul all this time and you just didn't know it. It's not like angels all look or act the same. If it's not a soul that makes us different, then what is it?"

In my hand, the cross melted into a pair of black angel wings. Barnabas was silent as he looked at them, and then he muttered, "I left heaven because I was forbidden to return, not because I was gifted with a soul."

Gift, I thought. I doubted it had even bothered him that he might not have a soul until Nakita said she had a sliver of mine, with the memories the black wings stole from me, memories of being afraid of the dark, of dying, of an end of everything. "Nakita said you were kicked out because you loved a human girl."

The back door to the Laundromat creaked open and an employee click-clacked out, checking to make sure the door was locked before heading for one of the nearby cars. Silent, we watched until her red Pinto roared to life and puttered away.

"Is that true?" I asked in the new silence. Barnabas didn't

say anything, his jaw clenched and his eyes looking black in the dark. Suddenly embarrassed, I let the angel wings shift back to the more familiar vision of a smooth rock. "I'm sorry," I whispered. "I'll shut up now."

God, what was I doing, prying into his past? He might look my age, but he was over three thousand years old to my seventeen. Like he really wanted to share *anything* with me.

"There were no timekeepers back then," he said abruptly, and I jumped even though his words were very soft, almost unheard over the nearby traffic's thrum. "Scythings were meted out by the seraphs, like they're doing now until things are settled with you. I was told to end the life of a girl whose soul was going to die. Pride was going to prevent her from asking forgiveness."

Barnabas shifted his weight, his hands clasped loosely over his drawn-up knees, but his eyes were not seeing the back of the Dumpster. The lost expression on his face was scary.

"The earth was so fresh back then," he said, the lines in his face smoothing. "Not this cement, carbon-polluted ember of what it's become. It was almost as if creation energy still rang in the rocks and echoed in the hum of the bees, or the breath of a child on the verge of becoming a woman, a woman so perfect that heaven was willing to cut her life short to bring her soul back to them unsullied."

I stifled a shiver, scared as to what he might say next.

"She was asleep in a field. My Sarah," he breathed, his shoulders easing as he spoke her name, giving it an odd accent. "Her name was Sarah, and I'd never seen anything more beautiful in all creation." His head dropped. "They should have sent someone stronger."

I wanted to touch his arm but didn't. How could I even pretend to understand? He'd laugh at me.

"I couldn't do it," he said, head down. "I . . . chose not to. I *chose*." Only now did he turn to look at me, frightening me with the intensity in his gaze. "Her soul was alive still, and beautiful. It seemed wrong to take it then. She woke, and I was standing over her with my scythe bared. She was so scared. I didn't want her perfect beauty remembering ugliness as she left the earth, so I lied. I told her she was safe, and I touched her, feeling her tremble. She believed me. I shouldn't have touched her. I might have been able to do it if I hadn't felt her fear."

He was smiling now, as if in a fond memory. "That she trusted me when I told her I'd do her no harm struck me to my core. I couldn't betray that trust, and my lie became truth." Barnabas's eyes tightened at the corner, and his clasped hands separated and pressed into the dirty cement. "A second reaper came to end what I couldn't, and I fought him, beat him, and sent him back broken to be made whole again in the forges of heaven."

His expression went sad as he looked at the dirty streets, seeing the past. "Her fate shifted in a single day because I saved her life." His eyes came to me as if I might deny it, but I could say nothing. "She realized she had worth when I saved her life, and her soul was renewed. Innocent, I left to tell the seraphs that fate could be swayed and to stop the scythings. They wouldn't listen, sending a third reaper even as I pleaded with them. She would have died if not for the guardian angels that happened to be with her at the time. They flocked to her. Her entire life, they clustered around her soul." His eyes went confused. "I never understood why. Now I wonder if it was so they would be there to save her life—after she saved her own soul."

My lips parted, and I wondered if Sarah's had been the first guardian angel. But what shook me was that he had changed a person's fate before and yet was reluctant to believe that it could be done again. Maybe it was because it happened so seldom.

Head tilted, Barnabas looked at me, his eyes still holding his love for her. "I refused to leave her after that, even when her soul remained intact and black wings couldn't find her when she died. So they kicked me out of heaven." His face changed, becoming harder as he threw a pebble to skip and hop through the parking lot. "It was worth it."

I sent my gaze to the busy road and the brightly lit apartment complex. "You stayed with her for her entire life?"

The faint sound of a siren came from the nearby interstate. Barnabas was smiling, a fond, soft smile that I didn't think I'd ever seen on him before. He looked seventeen to me, and I wondered how he'd handled looking that young for Sarah's entire life. But people hadn't lived much past forty back then. "Yes. I did," he said, seemingly embarrassed.

"And you say you have no soul," I said dryly as I threw a chip of cement at the Dumpster to hear it ting. "Good grief, Barnabas, if a soul is what lets us love, then you've got one."

He opened his mouth as if to protest, but then he stopped, his gaze going across the street as the sirens didn't fade but grew louder.

My heart gave a thump and I looked at my watch. It was almost nine thirty, but if there was trouble, Nakita would have told us. "It looks okay to me," I said, then sucked in my breath when the sound of breaking glass came loud over the traffic and a tongue of flame licked out of a third-story window, searching for the sky.

"Barnabas!" I exclaimed, scrambling up. My hand went around my amulet, and I looked at the street as the fire trucks and a cop car roared up. Puppy presents on the rug, it was happening. Where was Nakita?!

"Here we go," Barnabas said tiredly, and we edged out from behind the Dumpster.

"Tammy didn't come back, did she?" I asked, almost frantic. I couldn't take it if it had all been for nothing. "Barnabas, is she in there?"

"No. She's over there, but she's not inside. Johnny, either," he said, his eyes going silver for an instant as he touched on the divine, and my shoulders eased. "Your warning seemed to have changed her fate again—if not saved her soul."

"I haven't flashed forward to see it," I said, and we started toward the busy street, made twice as dangerous now that it was dark. There was a crosswalk, and Barnabas angled us to it.

"Maybe her soul isn't safe yet," Barnabas said.

"Maybe." That Tammy's soul might still be at risk was not a good thought. Barnabas pushed the CROSS button, and I fidgeted, wanting him to fly me across, but that would be hard to explain. We had time. If Tammy and Johnny were out of the building, we had time. Maybe now she'd listen to me. If Johnny didn't die, then she wouldn't give up on life, would she?

My fingers gripped my amulet, and I tried to relax enough to reach Nakita—if the fire trucks weren't enough of a clue. *Nakita,* I thought, closing my eyes against the DON'T WALK sign flashing across the six lanes of traffic, but Barnabas's shout jerked my eyes open and my attention shattered. My mental call for Nakita hit the ceiling of the air and broke, unheard.

"Black wings!" Barnabas said, his eyes wide.

My fingers on my amulet clenched, and I followed his pointing hand across the street. My knees seemed to wobble, and I reached for the light pole. Black wings. Scavengers of lost souls. If they were here, then there was probably a dark reaper on the hunt nearby. And if there was a hunting dark reaper, a light reaper was not far behind. *Damn it, did Ron flash and send someone?*

"You think they're here for someone else?" I whispered, and Barnabas shook his head as the slimy sheets of black glided like stingrays over the apartment complex. They looked like a shiny, silvery line from the side, and most people, when they saw them at all, thought they were crows. I wanted to believe it was coincidence, but the heartbreaking truth was more likely the seraphs had decided I'd mucked this up too far and had sent in the professionals. And here I was, stuck on the wrong side of the street.

Barnabas pushed the CROSS button again. The fire trucks were causing some confusion, and the light hadn't changed. Tammy was over there in that crowd—with half a dozen black wings circling overhead.

"Barnabas, we have to get over there!" I said, desperate as people started fleeing the apartments, dogs, cats, stereos, and TVs in their arms. A fireman was at the door keeping people from going back in for more as part of his crew went in to get the stragglers. And still the cars zoomed between us.

A boom of sound made me cower, mouth open as a huge gout of flame took one corner of the complex. "She isn't in there," Barnabas said, grabbing my arm. "I know it. Her aura puts her outside. She's outside, Madison!"

It was a small comfort. I looked up the road, then down. The smell of the burning building was thick, and the black smoke blocked out the stars. We didn't have time for this. "Let's go," I said suddenly.

"Madison! The cars!" Barnabas said, but I was already wiggling out of his grip and stepping off the curb.

Nakita! I thought, trying to touch her mind, my hand

holding my amulet in a death grip as the first car laid on the horn and screeched the tires, dinging the car next to it as it slid to a halt six feet in front of me.

Scared, I kept moving forward. The driver was screaming at me, but three lanes of traffic had stopped in a frightening sound of horns, skids, and a crunch of plastic.

My pace bobbled as the double image of Josh's house on a dark, deserted street overlaid itself on my reality of fire trucks and the three-story apartment complex. It was Nakita. I'd reached her. What was she doing at Josh's house? Waiting for him?

He's brushing his teeth, Madison, came Nakita's bored thought into mine as I saw through her eyes and she saw through mine, our connection that tight. *This might be a while.*

The apartment is on fire! I thought back at her, but she was already wide awake, having glimpsed my reality of another car slamming on its brakes only to be rear-ended and shoved forward another three feet, almost hitting me. I felt Barnabas take my elbow, shifting my path to avoid another car.

Madison, don't go in there! she shouted into my thoughts.

Scared, I wondered if I could enter a burning building and be okay. I was dead. I didn't need to breathe. *She's not in there, but there are black wings. Nakita, I need you!*

I looked up as Barnabas hesitated at the curb until I took the step up. Nakita saw the black wings through my eyes, and panic iced both of us at the memory of the pain of being eaten

74

alive. I held my amulet tighter. Black wings couldn't see me as long as I was wearing it. I was safe. *I was safe, damn it!* But it was hard to walk under them.

I'm coming! Nakita exclaimed, and the double vision vanished.

I took a deep breath, snapping myself out of the almost-trance. Barnabas was holding my elbow. Turning at the noise behind us, I blanched. Stopped cars were everywhere. Good thing the emergency people were here already. "Thanks, Barnabas," I whispered, knowing he had guided me through it. "Nakita was at Josh's. She's on her way. I'm not going to let a dark reaper kill Tammy. I won't!"

"And I won't let a light reaper give her a guardian angel," Barnabas said as his touch fell from me. "Not this time. I saved Sarah. Maybe I just need to try harder. Like you."

The strength of his words hit me, and I turned, surprised at his clenched jaw. He'd always supported me, but never had he looked this determined. It had to be the reminder of Sarah. "Thank you," I whispered, and he turned away, seeming embarrassed.

My attention went over his shoulder to the glow among the frightened people gathering in the parking lot of the apartments. I caught a flash of an amulet, then it was gone behind a wave of choking black.

"Look, it's Nakita," I said, eyes stinging as I started that way. But Barnabas jerked me to a halt.

"That's not Nakita," Barnabas said, his expression alarmed. "That's a dark reaper!"

My eyes darted back into the crowd, seeing nothing, then went back to Barnabas. "Crap," I whispered, feeling my knees go watery. "We're in trouble. Look, there's a light reaper, too. What in bloody heaven is going on? The seraphs know I'm here! Why are they interfering?!"

But it was obvious as to why. I'd really messed it up by saving Tammy's life.

Barnabas's lips pressed together as he watched the beautiful light reaper standing in front of the building, her hands on her hips as she looked appraisingly at the fire, not yet having identified who she was here to save. "It's Arariel," he said stiffly. "She's good. We're in trouble. She keeps guardian angels in her pocket. And the dark reaper? I recognize him, too. That's Demus."

Things were spiraling out of control. Clearly neither reaper had found Tammy yet, and though we could find her by way of her aura, so could Arariel if Ron had flashed and passed the description of it on to his light reaper. I'm sure the dark reaper had a description of her by now, too, thanks to the seraphs. And that is what ticked me off the most. The seraphs had written my attempt off without giving me a real chance. I was trying to fix this! They had no right to call in a dark reaper yet. Not yet!

But my hope was fading. Maybe they had given up on my ideas altogether?

"Maybe I can change Tammy's resonance," I said, barely

breathing the words, but I knew he had heard me despite the roar of the fire trucks and the calls of frightened people. "If Ron has flashed forward, he's given a description to his reaper, and if I can change it, she'll be safe."

"Do you think you can?" he asked, and I winced. "That's timekeeper magic. Even I can't do that."

"I don't know, but if we can get close enough to her, you can at least *shield* her resonance." But Tammy thought we were crazy, and she'd probably run if she saw us.

"It's worth a try." Barnabas's eyes flashed silver as he touched on the divine. "Found her," he said, hunching closer as if the surrounding reapers could read his mind. "She's scared. Alone. She's not in the parking lot. She's in an alley."

He turned, and I followed his gaze to a nearby self-serve storage site with rows of single-story buildings and garage doors. "There?" I asked him. It was noisy with the fire trucks' engines, and the lights from the emergency vehicles made come-and-go shadows on him as he nodded.

"Can you see her aura?" he asked me in turn, and I closed my eyes, trying to relax with the noise and commotion.

"No," I said. "Barnabas, I don't think that I can figure out how to change her aura." My eyes opened, finding him looking frustrated. "Let's just get over there and hide her resonance, even if we have to sit on her to keep her from running away."

He nodded, but as we turned to go, I saw a flash of amulet. I froze, my chest seeming to clench at the red hair and short stature. I'd never met any of my dark reapers except for Nakita, but by his unearthly beauty, I knew it had to be Demus. And as I watched him search the crowd for Tammy, anger kindled in me. This was *my* reap.

Taking a breath, I pulled myself straight. My eyes never left the beautiful angel who looked like he'd just gotten off a boat from Ireland. He was one of *my* reapers, and my hand gripped my amulet as determination filled me. He was going to do what I said.

"Go shield her, Barnabas," I said, and he grunted as he followed my gaze and saw Demus as well. "I'm going to go talk to Demus. Distract him at the least."

"Demus?" Barnabas said, looking shaken as his gaze darted back and away. "I know you're the dark timekeeper, but he's here on seraph business. He's not going to listen to you."

"The hell he isn't," I muttered. "I'm his boss."

Barnabas furrowed his brow and his eyes shifted to worry. "Madison—"

"Don't you Madison me!" I exclaimed. "I'm not going to let this go, and neither are you! Go find Tammy. Hide her resonance from the reapers. She likes you. I'm the one she thinks is crazy. I've got this! It's not like he can kill me!"

Barnabas stiffened. People carrying dogs and terrified cats stood between us and the dark reaper, shouting and gesturing about their lives going up in flames. The firemen ignored them the best they could as they worked, and the cops were trying to get them to go into the nearby skating rink. Smoke billowed between us, and when it cleared, Demus was gone.

Crap, where did he go? A black wing flew over, and we both ducked, the scent of decay and roses seeming to catch in my throat. "Madison!" came a familiar shout, and we turned to see Nakita elbowing her way through the frightened people. "Who is watching Tammy?"

A surge of pride came and went. She cared. Nakita cared about Tammy. If I could make a dark reaper care, then maybe this wasn't as impossible as everyone said it was. "Barnabas is," I said, and her wide eyes flicked at him, as if asking how when he was standing right beside us. "Nakita, you take Arariel," I said, pointing, then blinked when I realized that the light reaper in the black jumpsuit had seen us and had her sword bared and was grinning at us, waiting. "Don't let her put a guardian angel on Tammy, okay? Barnabas is going to hide Tammy's resonance and protect her. I'm talking to Demus."

Nakita nodded, her own smile eager as her hand gripped her amulet and her sword ghosted into existence in the other one. "With pleasure," she said, striding away, sidestepping a fireman oblivious to everything but his job. The stink of ash rose up, and I squinted through it, glad I didn't have to breathe.

I'd never seen so many black wings before, and the foul, mindless things swirled through the smoke to make it look like a living thing. Barnabas was still standing beside me like this was a lost cause. It would be only if we let it. "Will you go find

Tammy!" I exclaimed, and he looked at me, a sick expression on his face.

"It's too late," he said, and my heart gave a thump. "Look."

I followed his pointing arm to see Tammy standing at the top of one of the rows of the storage building, her mouth open and her dog in her arms, staring at the fire eating through the roof of her home. Demus was right behind her in the shadows, looking as if he was comparing her aura to something as his eyes went silver. In a blink between one flash of light and the next, his sword was made anew.

The memory of my heart pounded. "Demus!" I shouted, breaking into a run, dodging around crying people. "No!"

I could almost feel the whispers of feathers through my soul as I recalled being scythed, and the fear of waking up in the morgue with no way to change things, no way to hit the reset button and make a better choice. Tammy didn't deserve that.

"Madison!" Barnabas shouted, but I dodged around an angry man arguing with a cop and kept going.

Demus raised his sword, planning on taking her from behind, oblivious to me barreling down on him. "Wait!" I shouted, but he was swinging, and I plowed into Tammy, sending us and her dog sprawling into the shadows between the storage buildings.

She shrieked, and her dog barked furiously, but no one outside the alley heard. Still on the ground, I looked up. Demus's shock was turning into an ugly expression. His eyes dropped to my amulet, and he raised his sword again.

"You'll have to do better than that, light reaper," he said, mistaking me for an angel.

Well, that was one good thing, but then his arm descended in a smooth arc of motion. I pressed back into Tammy, wincing as I prepared to take the blow for her. I'd survive it. She wouldn't.

But the pure ting of the divine shocked through me, seeming to cut through the noisy confusion for a brief instant. My eyes cracked open. It was Barnabas, his sword inches from me and holding back Demus's blow.

"Barnabas?" the dark reaper stammered, still holding his position. "I thought you went grim." "Grim" was what they called reapers who didn't work for the light or the dark, mistrusted by both sides. They killed at random, or at least for a reason no one else could see.

With a grunt, Barnabas pushed him back. "I did."

His voice was flat, and again, I was taken by his image standing protectively over me, his duster mixing with the smoke, and his eyes dark and intent. Avenging angel, beautiful and unshakable. *Sarah, her name had been,* I thought, wondering how she had instilled in him the best of all of us.

I fell backward as Tammy scrambled out from under me and deeper into the alley. Her dog was gone, running into the crowd with his tail tucked. "Tammy!" I exclaimed, spinning onto my stomach and snatching her ankle. She fell, shrieking again, but at least Demus's blade went hissing harmlessly over her head as he swung at her. "Stay down!" I shouted at her, and this time she listened, eyes wide as she slid backward on her butt until she found a bright orange garage door.

"You talked to Shoe?" I asked. "You believe me now?"

Her eyes were fixed on Barnabas and Demus, and she jumped as their swords met and that sound rang out again. "You're crazy!" she exclaimed. "Freaking crazy! What the hell is wrong with you people?!"

Demus kicked at Barnabas, sending him backward. Tammy gasped as Demus turned to her, smiling wickedly. The eagerness in his expression was a dire warning. This was who I was supposed to convince to spare a mark's life? "And now you die!" he shouted, lunging.

"Demus, knock it off!" I exclaimed as I scrambled up.

I shot my hand out as he swung, his blade cutting right through me. Sparkles scintillated through me as heaven's might mingled within, then ebbed to nothing as it recognized me as one of its own and threw the divine strike back. My head snapped up, and I took a breath, feeling it go all the way to the bottom of my lungs.

Demus yelped, and when I looked, he was wringing his hand, his sword at his feet as he blinked in shock. "Who, by Gabriel's pearly toes, are you?"

"I'm your boss!" I said, still tingling from the blow, and ticked—even though it had felt good.

Demus bent to grasp his sword, and Barnabas shoved him.

Arms and legs flailing, the dark reaper smacked ungracefully into the wall.

"Barnabas, don't," I said, but the reaper had yanked him up, dazed and confused as he put him in a choke hold and spun him to face me. Using his foot, Barnabas kicked Demus's sword to me. I bent to pick it up, feeling the heavy weapon hum in my grip. It was responding to my amulet, I suppose.

"Your boss wants to talk to you," Barnabas said, his eyes pinched in anger. "Or didn't you get the memo?"

Demus focused on me, his snarl fading as his gaze flicked from the sword in my hand to Tammy crying behind me somewhere. "The dark timekeeper? Her?" His gaze dropped to my amulet, and then his eyes widened as he began to swear in Latin. At least I think it was Latin.

Looking vindicated, Barnabas let go of him, giving him a parting shove.

"You're the new dark timekeeper?" Demus said, the lights from the emergency vehicles flashing on him. "You're just a girl! Sweet seraph toes, no wonder the angels are still organizing the reaps."

My brow furrowed, and I came forward a step. "It kind of surprised me, too," I said, glad we were the same height and I didn't have to look up at him. "Listen, carrottop," I said as I handed his sword back to him, and Barnabas cringed. "I don't care what the seraphs said. You are not killing Tammy. She's off-limits. A test case, if you want."

Behind me, Tammy's sniffling stopped.

"But the seraphs . . ." Demus started, his glance going behind me to Tammy again. She shouldn't be hearing this, but it could only help her understand.

"The seraphs aren't playing fair," I said. "I bet they didn't even tell you what I'm trying to do, did they? This is *my* scythe, and they butted in by sending you, then Ron sent Arariel, is it? And now it's all messed up. But since you're here, you're going to do what *I* say, and *I* say Tammy is going to wake up tomorrow! We're trying to change her life, not end it."

It had been a mouthful, and I dropped back a step to catch my breath. Well, I really didn't need to, but still.

Demus was staring quizzically at me, then he glanced at Barnabas to see if I was joking. "You can't change a mark's path."

Barnabas was shrugging, and I said, "Not when you just kill them, sure."

Tammy started to edge for the opening of the alley. Barnabas moved to stop her, and she whimpered, standing with her arms crossed over her chest.

"We managed to change one person's life," Barnabas said. "We can do it again."

Demus fidgeted, his bared sword pointing downward. "The seraphs said—"

"I say she's off-limits!" I exclaimed. "Put your sword away and listen to me."

"Hell and damnation," Demus muttered, wincing as his sword vanished. "I can't just let Ron put a guardian angel on her. Do you know what happens to people who die who have lost their souls and fail to regain them?"

I didn't, but Barnabas seemed to relax, and after a quick look behind him, he put his own sword away. Hands now in his deep pockets, he eyed the burning apartment. "She'll regain her soul," he said softly.

Tammy made a dart for the opening past Barnabas, and the angel reached out, snagging her. "Let me go!" she shouted, smacking him, and he took the abuse, angling her so no one outside the alley could see her.

"This doesn't make any sense," Demus said, and I moved closer, hoping the nearby news van didn't look this way. "The mark either dies or gets a guardian angel. There's no other choice."

I smiled, hearing the word. "Demus, we are going to get along just fine. Choice is exactly what I'm going for here."

"I said let me go!" Tammy insisted, wiggling. "I have to get Johnny. I left him by the lamppost."

Looking almost cocky, Demus fluffed out his hair to get the sifting ash out of it. "Chill, babe, she just saved your life."

I exhaled. One reaper down, one more to go. The light reaper, though, wasn't going to listen to me. I should probably at least try to change Tammy's resonance, now that I had a moment to think.

"I said let me go!" Tammy screamed, and kicked Barnabas in the shin.

Howling, he dropped his grip on her. In an instant, she was gone. Barnabas took three running steps after her, then skidded to a halt. "You'll be okay?"

"Go!" I said, and Barnabas gave himself a quick shake. Turning, he vanished into the noisy mass of fire trucks and crying people. Damn, he looked good with his duster flowing and his eyes alight like that.

My attention turned to Demus. He was fiddling with his amulet, his eyes going silver for an instant before turning back to their original green. He was like a bright copper penny, beautiful and gold like Barnabas was beautiful and dark. "You're not like Nakita at all," I said, and he looked up at me, his white teeth startling.

"Well, you're not like Kairos."

I couldn't help my snort. "Thank God."

I came forward to stand at the opening between the two rows of storage buildings, my arms crossed. I was reluctant to step out of the somewhat peaceful spot. Beyond it was noise, lights, ash, billowing smoke, and spraying water.

"We're going to scythe her later, right?" Demus said. "This is just a way to make Ron crazy and put Barnabas off his guard?"

My head dropped, and I took a deep breath. *Two steps back.* Linking my arm in his, I started to lead him back into the mess. "Demus, we have to talk."

"There!" shrilled out a high voice, and we both turned, recognizing Tammy's voice. "There she is! She's the one that set the fire!"

My mouth dropped open, and I froze as Demus pulled away. Tammy was in a clear spot with a cop and a fireman. Johnny was with her, pressed into a scared-looking woman holding their dog. Their mom, maybe? Behind them trying to stay out of sight was Barnabas. There was a ting of divinity, and I saw Nakita, facing down the light reaper.

A strong thump came from my heart, then stopped. *She's blaming me for the fire? I'm the one that warned her to get out!*

"Puppy presents," I whispered, feeling Demus drop back and vanish into the crowd. I turned to make my own escape, but the cops were faster, and I found myself yanked around and staring up at a stern, smoke-marked face. God, he was big, and he had a gun.

"She broke into my house this afternoon!" Tammy was yelling, currently being held back by a second cop. "I called and it took you three hours to help me! I told you! I told you and you laughed at me!"

"I did not break into your house!" I said indignantly. "Your brother let us in."

It looked like the fire was almost out, but they weren't allowing anyone in yet. The parking lot was full of angry people, and they were all starting to look at me.

"She was talking about a fire," Tammy said, and the cop

holding me tightened his grip. "She told me not to be here tonight. Mom!" she exclaimed. "It's her! I'm telling you it's her fault! She said there was going to be a fire. How would she know unless she set it!"

"You . . ." the woman said, her fear finding an easy outlet. The dog in her arms squirmed, and she held him tighter. "You burned down my apartment? Why?"

Her shrill voice carried over the roar of the fire trucks, and I backed up to bump into a third cop. Crap, I was surrounded. Barnabas couldn't help. The cop looming over me grew even more grim. "What's your name, miss?"

"I want her in jail!" Tammy's mother yelled, attracting even more attention. "She set fire to my apartment! I lost everything. Everything!"

I touched the bump of my cell phone in my pocket, thinking of my dad. Oh, God, I didn't want him to get a call about me being two time zones away. "Uh, I have to go," I whispered, scared out of my mind.

I jumped when the cop gripping my arm pulled me to him. "I'm sorry, miss. Will you come with me?"

"She burned my apartment!" Tammy's mother said, starting to cry. "I've got nothing!"

You still have your children, I thought, but I couldn't say it. They wouldn't understand that Tammy's and Johnny's lives had nearly been lost.

"Hey!" I yelped when the cop pinched my arm and started leading me away. "I didn't set the fire! I just had a feeling."

"Yeah, well you and your feeling are in deep trouble," the cop said. "How old are you?" he asked. They couldn't question me without an adult present if I was a minor.

"Seventeen," I whispered, thinking of the disappointment in my dad's eyes. "Look, I shouldn't even be here."

The cop opened the door of one of the cop cars. It was quieter at the curb, the entire six lanes of traffic diverted somewhere else. People were everywhere. "What's your name? How can we reach your folks?" he asked.

I looked at the inside of the car and got in. My mouth was shut, and it was going to stay that way. I was so scared, but I was almost laughing. I was the dark timekeeper, able to stop time, stand down dark reapers, and fly with angels, and I was scared. Better to just go along with it until Barnabas showed up and changed their memories, but the less there was to change, the better. So I said nothing, looking up at him and knowing there would be no mercy.

He made a soft grunt. "Wrong answer," he said, then shut the door. It made a firm thump, cutting through the noise and confusion. Warm silence took me, comforting almost, though the seat was hard and the space tiny. Outside, the fire trucks thundered and people cried, but inside here, it was quiet.

The cop tapped the glass, and I jerked back. "You'd better

remember your phone number by the time I get back, missy," he said, his voice muffled. Turning, he walked away with a swagger.

"Big strong man put the little girl in her place," I muttered, crossing my arms over my chest and slumping back in the seat. I had a bad feeling I was going to miss my curfew. I could see Tammy talking to both the fireman and another cop, pointing at me. Her mother was in tears, and Johnny looked lost, patting his mom's knee as she sat on the ground and rocked their dog. Barnabas was lurking at the edge of the crowd, and Nakita. I didn't see Demus or the light reaper Barnabas had called Arariel. Maybe they were gone. Maybe all of this had changed Tammy's future.

Yeah, and maybe I've got ice-cream cones coming out of my ears. If the seraphs had sent a dark reaper, then Tammy's soul was still fated to be lost, and I'd accomplished nothing.

SIX

I watched the wall clock as I sat in the swivel chair, tapping my foot in time with its ticks to irritate the cop sitting behind the desk. But mostly I just sulked. Either luck or Grace had landed me here instead of the juvenile detention area, which was apparently full up at the moment. It could have been the fire, but I think it was Grace. My guardian-angel-turned-messenger had shown up halfway to the station, almost getting me into the psych ward when I started talking to her. Luck had stayed with me, so instead of a cell, I was stuck in some cop's office while they figured out what to do with me. It stank like stale cigarette smoke, and he had dried Diet Coke rings on his scratched desk. Nasty.

The somewhat overweight, stocky man looked up at me, and I gave him an insincere smile. Irritated, he set his pen down on his steel-and-laminate desk and crossed his arms over his chest, staring back at me. My cell phone was next to his oversize, ugly monitor. Grace had drained the batteries. She drained every single thing they tried to plug into it. They hadn't been able to contact my parents yet, and I hoped I'd be out of here before they managed it. Grace was good, but these guys were determined.

"You ready to tell me who that redheaded kid was with you?" he asked, and I shook my head. "How about how to call your folks?" he tried, and I looked at the ceiling.

"Punk-ass kids," he muttered, standing up and pocketing my cell phone. "We used to be able to put you gangbangers behind bars where you belonged and be done with it. You're only making it harder on yourself. We'll find out who you are. And that redhead, too."

"I didn't set the fire," I said, and he pressed his lips together, which made his mustache stick out.

"Stay there," he demanded, pointing a stubby, fat finger at me. "Don't touch anything."

I stuck my tongue out at him as he left, but he missed it, more intent on getting a sugar-induced coffee high. The frosted-glass door shut with a bang, and I jumped.

Exhaling a breath I'd taken who knew how long ago, I slumped back in my chair and swung my foot, looking over the cluttered shelves, the high, narrow window with the metal netting on it, and finally the scuffed green and white tiles. I didn't think my treatment was standard procedure, but I wasn't making things easy on them, either.

Head thrown back, I looked at the stained ceiling. I'd totally missed my curfew, and I was going to be so-o-o-o grounded when I got home, even if my dad never found out about this. But what really had me worried was Tammy. I didn't like that the seraphs had sent a reaper out to take her early. They *knew* I was handling this. Grace had told me that Barnabas was watching Tammy and that both Arariel and Demus were gone, so maybe my actions tonight in stopping Demus had caused them to reconsider. I just didn't know.

I'd feel a lot better if I could change Tammy's resonance to help hide her while I cooled my heels in juvie. Ron had changed mine several times, but he had done it by modifying my amulet, seeing as it was the source of my aura now that I was dead. Tammy didn't have an amulet to give her the illusion of an aura, so I'd have to change it some other way. Logic said I'd have to be with her to do it, but maybe all I needed to do was find her in the time line and just sort of . . . tweak it. It was worth trying.

Bringing my head down, I looked at the ticking clock. It was after ten, past midnight at home. My dad was going to kill me. "Grace?" I whispered, needing some company.

"There once was a cop shop in Baxter," the guardian-angel-turned-messenger sang out as she ghosted through the glass in the door, "who once a timekeeper did capture. Accused of a fire,

93

her condition was dire, but Barnabas won't let them ax her."

Looking at the bookcase of sloppy folders where she had landed, I squinted. "Grace? What's going on? I feel like I'm on a deserted island, here."

"You're in jail, Madison!" the angel said cheerfully. "The seraphs are angry. Tammy is a lost cause. And Demus is walking the streets again, looking for her. She's run away, just like the seraphs fated she would."

"What?" I sat up, now twice as worried for Tammy as I was before. "I thought Demus was recalled!"

The glowing ball of light landed on my knee, and a soft warmth soaked into me, like a sunbeam. "No, he just went back to heaven temporarily to make sure he wasn't doing something contrary to heaven's will by doing what you told him to do."

My face scrunched up into an ugly expression. "Three guesses as to how that went," I said sourly. "And the first two don't count." *Just like Tammy's desire to live, I guess. This is so unfair. I saved her from the fire. I saved Johnny from the fire, and still Tammy lets her soul die? What is wrong with the girl? Doesn't she see how much her mother and brother love her?*

"Um, they told Demus to get back down here and scythe her. Madison, it doesn't look good. He knows her aura signature and even what she looks like."

Thanks to me.

Grace rose up, the glow from her wings a spot of clean in the otherwise sticky office. "Barnabas and Nakita are going to get

94

you out," she offered, but I didn't feel much better. "Madison, maybe this isn't such a good idea," Grace said softly, and my heart gave a thump.

"Not you, too," I said, miserable. Damn it, why did no one believe that this was possible! We'd done it before. It would work if they would believe in it!

"It's just that the seraphs are so agitated!" Grace said, hovering right in front of me. "Their songs are going higher than I've ever seen them. The echoes are reaching down here, even. Those sensitive to it are getting visions. I haven't seen it like this since . . . since the Renaissance in Italy." She hesitated, and a burst of light came from her at a thought unshared.

"Maybe the seraphs shouldn't have butted in and sent Demus," I said, and Grace flew backward in alarm. "I'm trying to help Tammy!" I said, almost pleading. "It doesn't always happen whiz-bang! If it takes a year for a soul to give up on life, then it might take longer than two hours to rekindle the will to live. Scything someone to save their soul is so fast that it's cheap. Where's the honor in that? I'm getting better at this. Haven't I changed things already so that she is alive? Her and her brother both. She doesn't have that guilt now. How can that be a bad thing?"

Never. Never would anyone be able to convince me that Tammy and her brother dying in pain and agony in a fire was a good thing.

"There once was a brave human girl, immortality gave her

a whirl. For humans to save, God's wrath did she brave, her tenacity making me hurl."

"Nice." I looked at the door as a shadow went past. "Grace," I whispered, "I got this job for a reason. Maybe because I want to change things."

Her glow dimmed, and I felt cold as her depression soaked into the room. "What do the seraphs say Tammy's fate is now?" I asked. There had to be something I could do to make this better.

"It hasn't changed." A brief glow came from Grace, vanishing as she moved to the desk and stilled her wings. "Her brother's death had been the trigger of her soul's decline. Now it's losing her home in the fire. That's why they sent Demus back. She needs to come home early, or she's not coming home at all. Madison, we're talking about her soul. What is a human life compared to the everlasting soul? This isn't a game!"

"Is that what they think I think this is? A game?" I exclaimed, then lowered my voice before someone came in. "I want this to work so badly that it hurts. Tammy's fate hasn't changed at all?"

"Nope."

She sounded resigned, and I slumped back into my chair, not wanting to believe it. Barnabas could lie. Maybe seraphs could, too.

"Tammy's choice to stay with her brother tonight was based on fear, not a change in heart," Grace said. "You may have saved their lives, but Tammy still runs away, abandoning those who love her and losing hope in herself. Soon as Demus finds her . . ." Grace made a curious, high-pitched whistle, and went silent.

"Game over," I whispered, staring at the cop's desk and his phone. Maybe they left me alone thinking I'd use it and they could track my parents down. "Are you sure?"

"Yup."

I need to figure out how to change her resonance. I was a timekeeper, damn it. I should be able to do this. "Maybe if I talked to her a little more."

"Madison. Don't you get it? You are a timekeeper. You can't change fate. And you can't cause change. You see the future. You send out dark reapers to cull souls. If they are successful, the light reaper who failed escorts them to heaven's gate so the black wings don't eat their still-bright soul, severed early from their body. You know this. It's how you met Barnabas. And if the light reaper wins, a guardian angel keeps the mark safe in the hope that their soul will remember how to live. That's all you do!"

Screw it. I knew I could do more. "I see the future, huh?" I said, starting to get angry. "Then I want to see her future. Ask the seraphs to show me. I can still fix this!"

"They are angry at you! First you fix it so that they both die in grace, which is what they wanted, and then you go muck it up by talking to Tammy and getting her to leave the apartment. You may have saved both their lives, but you damned her soul doing it!" Grace said, glowing so brightly that she started to cast shadows. "I'm not going to ask them to do a far search on her!"

"Yeah? Well, I'm not too happy with them. Butting in like that." Sullenly I stood, pacing to the high window and back. That cop was going to come back. I had to get out of here. I had to find Tammy before Demus did. Jeez, what kind of time-keeper was I if I couldn't even elude a building of cops?

"I bet I can find her future by myself," I said, hands on my hips and glaring at her.

"See the future before the seraphs do?" Grace snorted. "There once was a girl with no brain, whose theories were kind of insane."

"Thanks, Grace. You're a font of wisdom," I muttered.

She rose up in a haze of glowing light, adding, "To outfly immortals, caused many to chortle. Because what the girl was, was vain."

"I'm not vain," I said as she hovered before the closed door. "I'm trying to get things done and no one is helping."

Grace bobbed up and down impatiently. "I gotta go. They found another phone battery."

"Go, go! And thank you," I said, waving at her as she flew through the glass and vanished. I didn't want to explain to my dad why I was on the West Coast and accused of arson. But even if Grace could keep them from contacting my dad, there was no way that I could hide that I wasn't at home. Never would I have imagined I could get things this messed up. Maybe Grace was right. Maybe they were *all* right.

Arms wrapped around myself, I glanced at the door and sank down in my squeaky chair. Maybe. But it didn't *feel* right. Barnabas had once said to trust my gut. My gut said this wasn't done. My gut said I could make this better. My gut said . . . I could make a difference.

I looked at the ceiling again, closing my eyes against the water stains that looked like swirling clouds or angels. *And I'm disgraced,* I thought, feeling a welling of self-pity. The seraphs were angry with me. Worse, I failed Tammy.

Ticked, I kicked out at the cop's desk. My toe met the thick steel with a dull thump, but I hadn't put any force behind it and nothing happened, not even a twinge in my toes.

I know Tammy's aura resonance. I can find her future by myself, I thought defiantly, but it was quickly followed by the realization that I probably couldn't. I wasn't being a self-defeatist—I was being a realist. Still . . . maybe I could change her resonance so Demus and Arariel couldn't find her. Buy me some time.

Resolving to try it, I looked at the ceiling again, exhaling everything out of my lungs. My eyes closed, and I pulled into my awareness the shimmering silver sheet of time that stretched to infinity in either direction. It glowed from the auras that comprised it, people that existed this very second. Falling from it like water or a drape, was the past. It still glowed, but not nearly as bright as the present. It was the light of collective memory. Go back too far, and the canvas grew black except for people that humanity had chosen to remember, silver triumphs and disasters that transcended time itself. But here, so close to the present, it was alight with color as lives intertwined, connected, and parted.

Going forward from the ribbon was vastly different. A black so intense as to almost not be there made a hazy patch of what-might-be. It was conscious thought, and it was what pulled us from the present into the future. It stretched wide in some places, and narrow at others, almost as if some people were living a tiny bit into the future by pushing their thoughts into it. Artists, mostly. Teachers. Children. The movers and shakers.

But it was the glowing ribbon of "now" that I was interested in, and I searched it, looking for Tammy. I knew Demus was likely looking for her, too, and a spike of fear almost broke me from my concentration. "Steady," I whispered, hearing a commotion down the hall. An argument about me, probably.

My mental sight grew clearer, and it was as if I hovered over the glowing blanket of light, searching for a particular note among an entire concert. Down one way, then retracing my steps and going farther down the other, searching among the thousands of souls near me. And then, like the small sound a vibrating glass makes when you run your finger across the rim, I felt her.

Tammy, I thought, elated. It had to be. She was alone by the looks of it, and not too far away. I focused on her, trying to put myself in her thoughts, but I only got the impression of wet hair, aching knees, and a sense of fear and hopelessness—of giving up and abandonment. The vibrating-glass sound grew louder, almost sour, and I wondered if it was this off-key sound/taste that the seraphs used to find souls in danger of becoming lost. It grated on me.

She wasn't thinking of the future at all, her thoughts pulling her into the next moment hardly stretching past her existence. I tried to slip my awareness into that dull gray haze that existed between everyone's present and future to try to reach her mind like I could Nakita or Barnabas, but it was like trying to thread a needle when you can't see the eye or feel the thread. I didn't think it was even possible. But changing the sound her aura was making . . . I might be able to change that.

A sliding thump in the distance jolted my eyes open, and I looked at the clock. Not even a minute had passed. Okay, I'd found her. Now to see if I could make a change. I shifted on the thin padding of the chair, trying to settle myself.

I willed my thoughts to slow and my focus to sharpen on my mindscape, making her aura my entire world and surrounding myself in her green and orange. I changed the color of my thoughts when I talked silently to Barnabas and Nakita. I really didn't know how I did it, apart from focusing on them and bringing them clearly into my thoughts: Nakita's willingness and desire to understand, Barnabas's deep-set melancholy for the human tragedy. But thinking of Tammy would only strengthen her existing aura, which was not what I wanted.

Frowning, I wondered if the answer might be in her past, and I looked down its length, seeing one sorrow layered over the next until it looked like that was all that existed for her: the birthday party her dad promised he'd come to, and then the argument he got in with her mother, which in turn took all the joy from the present he'd given her—and the purse he lovingly picked out for her was never used, forever stained with the memory of it.

There was the shame from a failed test, and another failed test, and another, until it was easier to pretend it didn't matter than to try, and to fail again. Deeper went the ugly words her friends spoke about another girl, but it was the knowledge that if they said such lies about one person, they probably spoke that way about her, too, which ruined any joy she might find with them.

But what tore at me was her understanding that the promises made in childhood were not true, that the lies our parents told us about being nice to others and others will be nice to you, that people were kind on the inside, and that love was more abundant than hurt . . . all of it was lies. No wonder her soul was lost. It wasn't that she had a harder life than others, but that she was blinding herself to the joy, that the little things were being brushed aside, forgotten. Her perception of good and bad was off because she refused to put the good on the scale, too.

And as I looked over her life, it was all I could do not to cry along with her. *What about this?* I thought, seeing the laughter in her mother's face when they had all come back to the shopping cart with the same carton of ice cream. *And this?* I wondered, watching Tammy scuff the marvel of a blue-jay feather under her shoe as she walked home. The satisfaction in a poem she wrote but never shared had to have more weight than the sigh of disappointment from her mother because of a dish-washer left unemptied—but Tammy ignored it, any satisfaction rubbed out as if it never existed.

And this! I exclaimed, seeing Johnny's smile of thanks when she put a bowl out for his breakfast. Was that worth nothing to her?

Tammy made a low moan, clutching her knees to her chest and rocking as if in pain. A flash of brilliance sparked through her aura, shifting the orange, and I knew that Tammy was see-ing what I was, not hearing my thoughts perhaps, but seeing the good in her life as I recognized it myself. Excitement shiv-ered through me as I realized her aura was shifting, the orange being muted, dulled, as I made her revaluate her life in small, subtle ways.

Encouraged, I focused on Johnny, and somehow, when everything else seemed to be blocked and useless, she remem-bered him, and her tears grew to include regret. It was the first step toward making a change, and I fastened on it like a lifeline. Rushing forward through her life, I found more memories of Johnny, forgotten. The sullen thank-you he gave her last Sun-day when she gave him the remote control instead of lording over the TV. The gratitude she had felt two weeks ago when she overheard him stick up for her with his friends. And the time that he changed her bowling score so it would look like she won. He loved her, and she had all but forgotten.

I could feel Tammy crying, holding her knees to herself, utterly miserable. I could feel her sorrow, her heartache. It ran through me like it was my own, and I gave her some of my hope, wanting to leave her with the idea that things weren't so bad. We were as much our past as our future, and hers was better than she knew. She just had to look at it in a new way.

A tear, hot and heavy, spilled down my cheek, and as I wiped it away, I pulled back from Tammy's aura to see what I'd done.

The orange at its center was now rimmed with black.

My heart gave a thump, then stopped. My first thought was that I'd damaged her, made things worse, but then I decided it didn't matter. Her aura had shifted, maybe just enough. Demus or Arariel wouldn't find her. Pulling back farther, I memorized Tammy's new resonance so *I* could find it again. I had no idea if the color shift was permanent or not. She was still a lost soul, but perhaps now she'd live long enough for me to get out of here and help her. I had to get her to do her own soul-searching. She had to make the choice herself.

Tammy's aura melted into the glorious bright line of the present as I withdrew, and a feeling of satisfaction filled me. Smiling, I fingered my amulet, warm from having touched the divine. *Take that, seraphs,* I thought, feeling empowered for the first time in a long while.

Curious, I brought my own resonance before me, wondering if I had any black in my aura before I had died and taken on the dark timekeeper's amulet. I felt a soft quiver in me as I ran my attention down my recent history, blurring over the snarl the time line had made when my soul had been cut out of it. It was where I had died, and it amazed me how the lives around me had bound together, supporting each other until a new weft and weave could mend the tear. And then the sudden burst of light when I had taken the amulet from Kairos, the timekeeper before me, using it to keep me connected to the present.

Nervous, I steadied myself and looked past the snarl. It wasn't easy to look at one's past, knowing it was fixed and one's emotions were laid bare. But I felt myself smile as I saw that I really hadn't changed since I'd died. Sure, my original aura of blue and yellow was vastly different from the deep violet that it now was, but my vision of the balance between good and bad was about the same.

It really was a pretty aura, I thought, sort of mentally running my fingers through it and feeling melancholy that it wasn't mine anymore. Or was it? Maybe I could change my own aura, just for a moment, and be myself?

Shifting focus, I ran my attention back to the present until I found myself sitting alone in a cop's office, waiting for them to find a battery for my phone. My aura was the dark of a time-keeper's, not my own, but as I compared it to the one in my memory, a faint glimmer of blue seemed to echo, not in my aura but in the hazy gray where the future became the now.

Between the now and the next? Oh, crap, I thought, excitement zinging down to my toes. Was that what the seraph had meant? Was that where my body was hidden? In the fraction of existence where time shifted from the past to the future? Time wouldn't exist there, and my body would be pristine and perfect, hovering an instant into death until I could reclaim it.

I took a deep breath, letting it all out to try to calm myself. If that was my original aura, then it had to be coming from my body, stuck in stasis where the old timekeeper had left it. I could reclaim my body, and with that, I didn't need the timekeeper amulet to keep me alive and the black wings off me!

It was all I wanted at this point, and I slowly centered myself, trying to focus on the small space. All around me were my thoughts reaching out to pull me into the future. And a tiny, almost-not-there glow of blue.

I snatched at it, wanting it so bad I could feel it. Vertigo came from everywhere, and I gasped, clenching the arms of the chair but refusing to open my eyes and lose what progress I'd made. "This is mine!" I whispered, feeling my lips move and the last bit of breath I had in my lungs escape.

There was the faintest taste of salt on my lips, and I licked them, curious. A faint breeze sifted my hair, tickling my cheek. But there was no air vent in the cop's office. The tickling grew more intense, and a faint, uncomfortable feeling of . . . of . . .

"I have to go to the bathroom," I said, eyes still closed and mystified. Since I had died, the only time I'd run for the bathroom was to evade a question from my dad.

An uncomfortable feeling slid through me, and my hands clenched on the arms of the chair. But they weren't gripping the hard plastic and metal. It was soft, like velvet.

My eyes flew open. Bright light stabbed into me, and I gasped. I was still sitting in a hot office smelling like cigarettes and stale sugar. But I was also in a breezy room, white curtains drifting in over the sills and thresholds. I could hear surf. And birds. The ceiling was marble, and the floor was black tile. I'd been here before. *My island?*

I looked down, seeing the grass-stained, torn remains of my prom dress overlaying the reality of my jeans and black lacy top covered in ash. My God! It was my body! I had found my body between the now and the next right where the seraph had said it was. I wasn't in it yet, since I could still see the reality of my blue jeans and black top, but I had found it. And the best part? My body looked okay. It had been stuck frozen in time, and it was normal. Now all I had to do was let go of the body I was in and . . . take it.

"Madison!"

Someone grabbed my shoulder from behind. I jerked, and with a cry, I felt a gut-wrenching pull. Pain vibrated through me, and I doubled over, eyes closed against the pain. The sound of the wind and the taste of the salt were gone. I had almost had it, but now it was gone!

"Madison! Are you okay? You looked like a ghost! See-through!"

"Stop!" I croaked out, almost vomiting as I bent over my knees. My eyes opened, and sadness rose up. I was staring at the ugly green and white tiles of the police station. Where in the hell was the beach?

"I almost had it!" I cried, standing up and nearly hitting Barnabas in the chin.

He backed up in confusion, and I spun, looking at the chair as if I might still see myself sitting in it, torn prom dress and all. But all that I saw was the empty chair.

"Barnabas, I was there!" I pointed down, feeling my heart thump, but I knew it wasn't real. It wasn't real—and the heart-ache of that almost brought me to tears. "I found my body. Between the now and the next! It was at the island, stuck in a time bubble or something! Barnabas, damn it! Why couldn't you have waited just a few minutes more! I almost had it! I was in it. I was almost alive!"

Barnabas's shocked expression went empty. "You—"

"Found my body! Yes!" I looked at the ugly room, torn between crying and screaming at someone.

There were footsteps in the hall, and Barnabas took my elbow. "Let's go. The sooner we get out of here, the fewer memories I'm going to have to fix."

He started pulling me to the door, and I dug my heels in.

Memories? He's worried about memories? "I found my body, and you don't care!"

"I do care, but we have to get out of here!" His grip on me tightening, he jerked me into the hallway as someone skidded around the bend in the hallway.

"Where do you think you're going?!" the cop said, and then his eyes widened as he looked at Barnabas. "Hey, weren't you at the fire?" Falling into a crouch, he reached for his gun.

"You have got to be kidding me," Barnabas said, pushing me toward the end of the hallway.

"I found my friggin' body, and you don't care!" I insisted, resisting.

"Stop!" the cop exclaimed, and Barnabas's eyes, inches from my own, glinted silver. As sweet as syrup, the man fell down.

I looked over my shoulder to see, but Barnabas's grip on my arm tightened, and he started pushing me to the end of the hallway again. "I'm thrilled you found your body, but we're trying to get out of here," he muttered. "You can claim your body later." His gaze went over my shoulder, and his eyes widened. "Run!"

He shoved me, and I staggered, almost cracking my nose as I went down on all fours. My palms stung, and my knees throbbed. I looked up in time to see Barnabas make a gesture, his eyes silvering for a moment.

The second man bending over the first fell, but I could hear more people coming. Ticked, I pulled myself up off the floor.

My palms were sticky, and I didn't know what to wipe them on. "Later?" I shouted. "I want it *now!*"

My last words were a veritable shout, and a wave of angry force pulsed from me.

Swearing, Barnabas ducked, his face white as he rose from his crouch and looked at me.

I staggered as the dizziness that had risen up and lapped about my head slowly ebbed to my feet. My hand went to the wall, and I swear, it felt spongy. I yanked it back, then blinked. My stone had gone ice cold and silvery.

"Uh, Madison?" Barnabas whispered, and I realized it was quiet.

You know . . . too quiet.

The men sprawled on the floor weren't moving. Fear trickled through me as I remembered that burst of anger that had exploded from me. Had I killed them?

"Whoo-hoo!" came Nakita's excited whoop from somewhere in the building, and a sudden pounding of feet echoed in the hallway. I spun as she leapt over the downed men, skidding to a breathless halt, her sword bared and her amulet gleaming. "Madison, when did you learn to stop time?"

Stop time?

"I, uh," I stammered, then looked at my amulet. It was still silver, like Barnabas's eyes when he touched the divine. A thread of sound was running through me, and when I chanced a look at the time line, it burst into existence so brilliantly that I almost fell.

"I don't know," I said, instinct making me cover my eyes, though the brightness was in me. Blinking, I dropped my inner sight, and looked up. Barnabas was holding me upright. Seeing me okay, he let go and stepped back. "Uh, how do I undo it?" I asked them.

"Not yet!" Nakita exclaimed, her color high. "Wait until we get out." She darted past us to the back door, sending her whoops of excitement to echo in the absolute stillness. The clock in the cop's office wasn't ticking when we passed it. The lights from the cars outside weren't moving. The only sound in the entire world was coming from us. It was as creepy as all get-out. *And I did it?*

"Let's go," Barnabas said, clearly subdued.

I followed him down the hall to where Nakita was pushing open the automatic door. Outside was even creepier, with no wind, no noise. It was as if we had walked into a painting. Everything felt flat. Nakita almost danced down the cement steps and to the shadowed parking lot. "Madison, you're getting good at this. I think we should try teaching you how to make a sword from your thoughts when this is done, okay?"

I cringed. All I wanted to do was go home. I wanted to get my body and go home and forget everything that had happened. But if I did, nothing would change. Not in heaven, not in earth, not in me. Nothing.

"How do I start time?" I whispered, confusion so thick in me it made me ill.

"I don't know." Barnabas scuffed to a halt beside a cop car, turning to look as a ball of light burst out the still-open doors.

"Madison!" Grace exclaimed, darting circles around me. "You stopped time? That's wonderful! And how clever of you to exempt the divine!"

I had been wondering about that, but it wasn't as if I knew what I was doing.

"It would be if she knew how she did it," Barnabas said, echoing my thoughts. He stood with his hands on his hips, watching Nakita doing her impression of a professional football player after a touchdown.

"What is your problem, Barney?" Nakita said, giving him a little shove as she finished. "Madison is finally getting the hang of this. You look like you just swallowed a scarab."

Barnabas furrowed his brow, the skin tight around his eyes. "She found her body."

Nakita's smile hesitated, her eyes becoming confused even as her delight lingered in her expression. "What?"

"She found her body, between the now and the next," he said again, and even Grace's glow dimmed.

It was if the deadness of the world around us seeped into Nakita. She froze, unspoken thoughts turning her elation into ash. "Nakita," I said, reaching out, and she took a step back, the sword in her hand dissolving into nothing. Her amulet went dark as the energy was reabsorbed, and her gaze fell from mine.

"I'm happy for you," she said, not looking at me. "I know it's what you wanted."

"Nakita . . ." Why was I feeling bad about this? If the seraphs weren't going to give me a real chance to make this work, then why should I stick around and be a part of a system that I didn't agree with? I could be with Josh then, and be normal. But she had turned away, and guilt hit me hard.

"Nakita!" I said more firmly, and she stopped. Feeling like a heel, I caught up with her and tried to get her to look at me. "I don't want to give this up, but what choice do I have?"

"You say you believe in choice," she said, turning away. "But you don't really. Or you'd stay."

Again she turned away, and this time I let her go. Grace came to hover over my shoulder, and Barnabas eased up on my other side. "Why does everyone think I should stick around when no one believes I can change things?"

"I believe you can change things," Barnabas said, but I wasn't listening, and I stomped off. Nakita had found the street and was walking in front of cars that had been going fifty miles per hour, her pace stiff and her arms swinging. "I do," he insisted as he caught up to me. "That's why I left Ron. I still think you can if you'd stick with it."

He probably did, which made it all the harder.

"Madison," he said as he drew me to a stop. We were at

the curb, and the lights from the oncoming traffic lit his face, showing his pinched brow and his eyes, pleading with me. "You keep saying that no one is giving you a chance to see if your theories work, but they are. You're trying to change a system that has been in place since people looked up at the stars and wondered how they got there. It works for a reason, and you might make more progress if you'd take the time to see why a system is in place before trying to change it to yours. The seraphs are singing. I can hear them even down here. Change is happening; you simply don't see it. You might have to do something you don't want to for a while before you find the way to make your change happen."

I couldn't say anything back, I was too depressed. Seeing me silent, he inclined his head, then turned to follow Nakita, walking fast as he tried to catch up.

"Nakita!" he called out, and I stared at him, my hand wrapped around my amulet. I think it was the longest thing he'd ever said to me, and it left me feeling even worse.

"I'm such an idiot," I whispered to Grace.

"But you're *our* idiot," she chimed out, and I winced.

"What do you think I should do?" I asked as I started to follow them, my sneakers barely lifting from the asphalt.

"First, you need to let go of the time line and start things moving," she said, "before Ron comes to see what's going on."

"Yeah." Okay, let go of the time line. How does one do that?

"And I think you ought to go home and check in with your

dad before he realizes I set his clocks back two hours," Grace added. "He thinks it's . . . like, ten thirty. Same as here."

"Oh, wow. Thanks, Grace." The first inkling of hope started to seep back in, and I mentally added *talk to Nakita* to my list of things to do. She looked positively melancholy as she walked beside Barnabas, her head down as he talked to her.

"Well, once a guardian angel, always a guardian angel," she said wryly, if a glowing ball of light could be wry. "And after that, you can meet us back in the graveyard to figure out how to fix this mess you made with Tammy. The seraphs are ticked. When did you learn how to change a person's aura?"

"Right before I learned how to stop time," I said, thinking it wasn't right that my learning something had gotten me in trouble with the seraphs. Again.

"Great," Grace said pointedly. "How about starting it back up? This is getting old. Any tighter of a grip, and you would have stopped your reapers, too."

I nodded, bringing up the image of the time line in my imagination. It was brighter than usual, and it was starting to give me a headache. *Relax,* I thought, dropping my shoulders. My eyes flashed open when, just that easy, the noise and color rushed back into the world.

"Good job!" Grace said, dipping up and down as car lights flickered over us and a cry of outrage rose up from the cop shop. "Let's get out of here."

I ran after Barnabas and Nakita, glad time was going again,

but that lingering feeling of doubt wouldn't leave me. Yes, I had found my body, but no one seemed to care. Or rather, they wished I hadn't. What did it say about my life when the thing I wanted most of all was the very thing that would cause me to lose the things I loved?

SEVEN

It was almost too dark to see when Barnabas back-winged and landed me gently on the roof of my house, the threat of rain making it darker than it typically would be. The muffling black was like a blanket, smothering. It seemed to spill out my darkened bedroom window to fill the entire world and make one big nothing. It was sort of how I felt inside.

My short hair flew up as Barnabas settled his wings, and I reached to smooth it, catching a glimpse of his wings before they vanished. Head down, he stood before me as if wanting to say something.

It had been a very quiet flight back—my thoughts on Nakita, his on who-knew-what. Leaving her had been hard, with her stalking to the graveyard to wait for me, probably thinking I was going to abandon her once I got my body back. Demus was somewhere this side of heaven, but since he was looking for the wrong resonance, I had a space of time to regroup. I was going to spend at least five minutes of it convincing my dad that nothing was going on and that I was going to bed.

There was that word again. Nothing. Nothing was exactly how I felt. Empty inside. After having been in my body for even that instant, I remembered what it was like to see, feel . . . to really be a part of existence. Now the shell that my amulet gave me felt like the nothing that it was.

"You sure you want me to leave?" Barnabas finally said, seeing as neither of us was moving from the roof.

I nodded, arms wrapped around myself, the slight chill seeping into me after the steamy warmth of Baxter. "It should only take an hour," I said, wondering why he'd landed here instead of the front yard. "And I want to see if Josh can slip away. It'd be great if he could come back with us." He, at least, would be glad I had found my body. And that it wasn't a mass of decayed yuck.

"An hour." Looking uncomfortable, Barnabas flicked a dark gaze to me, then back to the cloudy skies. "I've got time to go back and get your phone, then. There's no reason to leave it there to trigger memories."

"Thank you," I said earnestly. I hoped he'd get it. There was no way to explain to my dad why it was in California.

"Unless you're sure you don't want me to wait for you?" Barnabas asked.

I shook my head. Nakita was there alone. Moving to the edge of the roof, I sat down to make the jump to the ground. Lucy, the neighbor's golden retriever, wasn't in the yard. I hesitated at the scrape of Barnabas's sneakers beside me, and I looked up to his shadowed face.

"What do you want me to say to Nakita?" Barnabas asked, his eyes catching the glow from the streetlamp. "She thinks you're leaving. Are you? You want me to lie to her?"

My depression thickened, frosted with guilt. I didn't know. I wanted to stay, but I couldn't do this if all I was doing was killing people. "Tell her that I'm thinking," I said, unable to look at him anymore. "Tell her that I'm proud of her, and you, and that I want it to work. I want to stay. I *will* stay if . . ."

Barnabas didn't move, but somehow, he became darker. "What if the seraphs don't allow you to do things your way? They did send Demus."

It was exactly what I was worried about, but I gave him a fake smile, my feet dangling into the black between heaven and earth. "Hey! I'm the dark timekeeper. What are they going to do? Kill me? They already did that." I looked away, fear making me drop my eyes. They could take my amulet away and let black wings destroy me. A soul without an aura was fair game, and mine came from my amulet right now. But I wasn't going to take the job of dark timekeeper and send reapers out to kill people to save their souls if the reason I was doing it was because I was afraid. Even if I was.

"I'll talk to her," he finally said, clearly seeing my fear.

"Thanks, Barnabas." I pushed myself off the roof, my knees bending to absorb the impact of the fall. I looked up to try and see him wing out, but there was nothing except the barely moving black branches between me and the heavy clouds. Head down, I walked to the front door, looking at my shoelaces. Skulls and hearts. Maybe I should grow up.

A sliver of self-preservation made me hesitate before I went in. Grace said she'd fixed things with my dad, but it was still hard to grab the doorknob and turn it. Reaching for it, I felt a prickling through my aura. My fingers curled under, and I waited, breathing in the feeling.

"It's almost like . . . I'm being watched," I said, then spun as my amulet grew warm.

My breath hissed in, and I watched a vertical line of divine silver crack the night. A somewhat short, thin man seemed to step through it sideways, the light making a silhouette of his tight, graying curls and his billowy clothes.

"Ron," I hissed, exhaling everything I'd just taken in.

It was the light timekeeper himself, standing on my front lawn in the dark. My first thought to call Barnabas lit through me and died. I could stop time, damn it. I didn't need Barnabas's help. Besides, he was probably shielding his resonance and wouldn't be able to hear me. Cocking my hip, I stared at Ron as he finished materializing.

"What do you want?" I shot out, and he jerked his head up,

seeming to be surprised I knew he was there. It was a brief flash of satisfaction in an otherwise sucky night.

The small man quickly recovered his pompous attitude, shaking out his billowy robes that were more suited to the back lot of a Hollywood set than anything that had to do with reality. And he thought what I wore was funny? "To know what you're up to?" he said, filling those few words with more sly bile than one would think possible. God help me, he knew everything.

My arms crossed over my middle. I didn't care if it made me look vulnerable. My day hadn't gone well, and there was no hiding it. "I'm trying not to get grounded," I said lightly. "Maybe you should leave before I yell for help and get you thrown in jail for being a pervert."

Ron only smiled that same, infuriating smile. "You learned how to stop time. Congratulations."

Funny how it didn't sound like "congratulations" when he said it, and I looked at the porch light, wishing Grace was here to make a tree branch fall on him. "Yeah? So what?"

Ron took a step closer, head cocked as he lost his smug air. "I had a reaper out there."

"So I noticed." I rocked back toward my door, not liking this.

"So I wonder what you're doing . . ." he drawled as if I'd fill in the blank.

"Blah, blah, blah," I said, making talking-hand motions.

"Don't start monologing, Ron. I'm not doing anything." I turned to go inside, gasping when Ron grabbed my arm. Spinning, I yanked out of his grip, shocked that he had touched me.

"Back off!" I exclaimed softly as I stared down the two steps at him, not wanting to explain to my dad who he was. My heart gave a thump and settled.

"You changed the mark's resonance," Ron said, clearly angry as he looked up at me. "My reaper can't find her."

Wahh, wahh, wahh, I thought. *Madison isn't playing fair!* But what came out of my mouth was a short "Good."

"You're going to get her killed!" Ron said.

My eyes narrowed. "Did that," I said shortly. "Made a video. Posted it online. It's over, Ron. Go home."

"It is not over," he insisted, looking both angry and confused. "She isn't dead. You wouldn't kill her. Though I don't know why. What are you trying to do? You can't change things. They are what they are."

I took a breath, feeling the disappointment of the entire day fall on me. But this time, it only made me mad. I didn't have to explain myself to him. Yanking my door open, I went inside, grimacing at him standing at the foot of the steps before I shut the door in his face.

Exhaling, I leaned back against it. I could hear my dad on the phone in the kitchen, his voice holding a hint of strain as it rose and fell. I pushed myself up and peeked outside through the narrow window beside the door. Ron was gone. Thank you, God.

The house looked quiet and normal, and my dad stepped from the kitchen with the landline phone stuck to his ear. My first thought was he was on the phone with Josh or Josh's mom, wanting to know where I was, but then he gave me a finger wave and I knew he thought it was still before my curfew.

"Bev, she's fine," he said somewhat crossly, and I realized he was talking to my mom. "It was just a prank phone call."

Oh, jeez. The cops at the juvie center had reached her. Worried, I glanced out the window for Ron, then came in, trying to hear her end of the conversation.

"I said, she's fine!" my dad said, rolling his eyes at me. "She's upstairs asleep, or I'd put her on the phone so you could see for yourself."

I reached for the receiver, and he shook his head. *Why is my dad lying to my mom about where I am?*

"Bev," he said, his voice taking on that tightness that I remembered from when I was growing up. "Listen to me. Madison is fine. I am fine. We are getting along fine, and I think *you* have a problem with that. I can raise our daughter just as well as you can. She's a wonderful girl, and I honestly don't know where you come up with this stuff. I'll have her call you tomorrow. I'm not going to wake her up because someone is yanking your chain. Go take a valium or something."

My eyes were wide as he hung up and exhaled, looking at the phone like he wanted to throw it at the wall. "Mom?" I asked, though it was obvious.

"She thinks I can't take care of you," he said, the skin around his eyes wrinkling to make him look tired.

A sick feeling seemed to steal around my heart, and seeing it reflected in my eyes, he forced the irritation from his expression, smiling, though I knew he was still upset and likely would be for a few days. "Dad, you're taking care of me great," I said, feeling lost, and I gave him a hug, my guilt rising high. My dying was not his fault, and I couldn't bear it if he thought it was.

He gave me a squeeze, then he stepped back. "Thanks," he said softly. "Call your mother tomorrow. Trust me, you don't want to talk to her now," he said as he went back into the kitchen to hang up the phone. "Someone told her you were on the West Coast in jail, having been accused of setting fire to an apartment complex."

"Really?" I said, forcing a laugh as I wondered how a call had gotten past Grace.

My dad carefully hung up the phone, but his fingers were shaking, and the click seemed unusually loud. "Maybe if your mother would get into the twenty-first century and get caller ID, she wouldn't have to put up with cranks like that."

Yawning, he covered his mouth with the back of his hand. "I can't believe how tired I am," he said, dropping his wrist to look at his watch. "I tried to call you but you're either out of minutes or your battery is dead." His eyes met mine, annoyance in them. "Again," he added.

I couldn't bear lying to him, and I went to the fridge, pretending to get a glass of apple juice. I dumped out about a gallon of it every week. "Um, it's probably the battery," I said as I stuck my head in the fridge and breathed in the cold air. "I, uh, kind of loaned it to Barnabas."

"Madison!"

The exclamation was like a whip, and I pulled back out of the fridge, my eyes downcast. "I'll get it back tomorrow," I promised.

"Use mine until you get yours back, okay?" he said as he handed me his. "Where did you and Josh eat?"

The heavy black phone felt funny in my grip, different from my slim pink one. The time was more than two hours off, but as soon as I looked at it, it magically shifted to the right time.

"Um, The Low D," I said, scrambling to remember our cover story. "Nakita and Barnabas were with us. After Josh's track meet stuff."

"You ate, right?"

"As much as I always do." Smiling, I got a glass out of the cupboard and poured myself some juice. He wasn't saying anything, just looking at me with concern. "I might have something before I go to bed, though," I added, and he seemed to lose much of his worry. "Can I go over to Nakita's tomorrow?

We took a lot of pictures at the meet and I want to help her organize them."

"Sure, but get your chores done *before* you leave this time," he said. "I might not be here when you get up. I've got to go in tomorrow to close out a trial. I hate those ten-day biological runs. Half the time you either have to start them on the weekend or end them on one. Don't forget to empty the dishwasher. Take out the recyclables. And I want the porch swept before you leave. Front and back this time."

It was the usual list, and I recapped the juice, hoping he would leave before I had to drink some. "Yes, Dad," I almost groaned.

Again he yawned, looking at the clock over the stove. "I can't believe how tired I am. I must not have had enough coffee today."

"I'm going to bed, too," I said, leaving my juice on the counter and going to give him a hug good night. His arms went around me in a blanket of security, and he kissed the top of my head.

"I'm serious about calling your mom tomorrow," he said softly, still holding me. "She's worried about you."

"I will," I promised.

He let go and I dropped back. Turning to leave, he hesitated. "You smell like smoke."

I didn't know if he meant from the fire, or the cigarette stench from the police station, and I fumbled, saying, "I got a ride home with one of Josh's friends. The car stank."

My dad accepted that, smiling faintly as he rubbed the top of his head, leaving his hair mussed. "Did you set your stops right?" he asked, meaning the photography stops.

"You know it!" I said cheerfully.

"I want to see the pictures when you're ready," he said as he turned and shuffled into the hall. "I know it's the weekend, but don't stay up too late!" he said from the stairs.

I exhaled, my faith in Grace increasing a hundredfold. Damn, she was good at keeping me out of trouble with my dad. She and Josh both. "Okay!" I called back to him, then stood there, listening to hear his bedroom door shut. Maybe I could get out of here sooner than I thought.

The house went quiet, and I dumped my apple juice, rinsed out the glass, then hesitated when I opened up the dishwasher. Sighing, I pulled the rack out and started to empty it. I was able to stop time, and here I was, emptying the dishwasher. It might not be a bad idea to sweep the porch, too, before I left.

The soft tap at the kitchen window shot through me like a pulse of fear, and my head snapped up, thinking it was Ron. But it was Josh standing between the house and the foundation plantings, his nose and eyes showing. Seeing my relief, he dropped from sight, but I was already on my way to the front door, swearing softly at him for having scared me.

"Josh!" I whispered as I opened the door. "I thought your mom grounded you!"

His gaze went to the stairway, and he whispered back, "You're not the only one who can sneak out. What happened? Did you get in trouble? My mom tried to call your dad, but the call wouldn't go through, and then the phone died."

I exhaled, thanking Grace. She loved causing mischief if it would keep me out of trouble. I pulled him in, seeing the street behind him was empty and dark. He must have biked over so his car wouldn't wake anyone up. "Come on in," I said softly. "My dad's upstairs."

"No doubt." Josh looked at his watch. "You're going back to Baxter tonight, right?"

I nodded, not sure what I hoped to accomplish anymore, but knowing that it wasn't over yet. "I'm going to have to. Josh, you won't believe what happened."

He followed me in, taking the plates from me as I pulled them out. Josh knew my kitchen almost as well as I did, and he slid them away, being careful not to make too much noise. "Did you get grounded?" he asked in a serious voice.

I looked up from stacking the bowls, blinking until I figured it out. "Oh! No," I said. Grounding was the least of my worries. "Grace set the clocks back. My dad thinks it's before midnight. No grounding."

"Nice!" he said, glancing at the clock over the stove as I went to reset it. "What's so awful, then?" His face went concerned. "Oh, no. Madison, they didn't . . . die, did they?"

I touched the digital clock, and the numbers jumped to the

correct time. I jerked my hand back as if stung, staring at it. *That was weird.* "No," I said. "The apartment caught on fire. Tammy and Johnny are okay, but she told the cops that I set it. I spent most of the night in some cop's office watching Grace short out my phone's battery so they couldn't call my dad."

Josh made a noise of disbelief, and I turned, shrugging. "Barnabas and Nakita got me out and I learned how to stop time *and* change Tammy's aura."

"That's great!" Josh said, his pleased expression fading when I didn't smile back. "Isn't it?"

"The seraphs sent a dark reaper to scythe Tammy," I said, feeling the hurt of that all over again. "They're giving up on me. So of course Ron sent a light reaper to stop him. It was a mess. He stopped by tonight. Ron, I mean." I looked toward the front door as if I could see through the walls. "Trying to figure out what I was doing."

Eyes wide, Josh fumbled for a clean glass. "So what is he going to do?"

"I don't know," I said, the open dishwasher between us. "At least he admitted he doesn't think I'm trying to kill her." *No, he just thinks I'm being stupid.* "I did manage to stop the dark reaper the seraphs sent out. His name is Demus. He's a redhead," I said, my focus blurring as I remembered how good he looked.

"What, do you like him?"

Josh's voice had risen in pitch, and I jerked my attention to him. "He's an angel," I said, hiding a quick smile when I realized he was jealous. "You're not worried, are you?"

"Of an angel? No," he said, but his motions as he stacked the bowls said otherwise.

"Josh . . ." I said, worried that he felt like he didn't belong and might leave. "Angels are pretty, but they are kind of intense, you know?"

"Yeah, but they can fly."

"Oh, stop it," I said, giving his shoulder a little push as I leaned across the dishwasher between us and grabbed the silverware. "I like you, okay? Not an angelic serial killer."

"When you put it like that . . ." he said, smiling, and I turned away, suddenly uneasy. Angelic serial killer, and I was the boss. As soon as Josh figured out how true that was, he might be gone, and then I'd be a bigger freak than before. Puppy presents, this sucked.

Silverware in hand, I yanked the drawer open with my pinkie. Tonight had been a disaster. I couldn't plug the holes fast enough, and the water was almost up to my chin. Frustrated, I gave up sorting the forks from the spoons, and just dumped them in and shut the drawer. Arms over my chest, I stood at the counter and stared at the wall.

"You'll make it work. I know you will," Josh said softly.

The dishwasher was empty, and feeling numb, I sat at the table and put my head in my hands. I couldn't do this anymore. The lies, the sneaking around. I was trying to change something that no one else wanted to change—no one else saw anything wrong with. Except Barnabas. Barnabas believed I could do it.

Head down, I exhaled, feeling my breath leave me and my lungs collapse. I didn't have to breathe again, and that bothered me. I wanted to be normal, damn it. What guy wants to date a superhero who never needs rescuing? He had his pride. Besides, the seraphs didn't believe in me. Tammy hated me. Nakita was upset. My eyes grew warm, and I wasn't surprised when a tear brimmed and fell. *I don't have to breathe, but I can still cry? How unfair is that?*

"Madison?"

Josh's hesitant touch on my shoulder made me even more depressed, and I sniffed, not looking up.

"I'm sorry," I said, sitting up and wiping my eyes. "I'm not crying," I said as if trying to convince myself, because I sure wasn't convincing him. "It's only that nothing is going right anymore."

Smiling faintly, Josh sat down beside me. "It's going to be okay," he said, finding and holding my hand.

"That's not why I'm crying!" I said, head down and tears leaking out no matter how hard I tried to stop them. "I mean, Tammy is important, but . . ."

I couldn't say the words. They sounded so lame next to the problem of Tammy being hunted by a dark reaper. One of *my* dark reapers.

"Then what?" Josh asked, and I looked at my hand in his. He was holding it protectively, and it hit me hard.

"I-I found my body," I whispered, looking at our hands on our touching knees. "When I was in the police station. I almost had it, almost managed to slip into it completely and make it mine again, but Barnabas came in, and I lost it."

"Your body?" Josh said, then glanced at the hall. "Madison, that's fantastic!" he said, his voice softer. "Why are you upset? If you found it once, you can find it again. You can be fully alive again! That's great!"

"It's not great," I said, miserable. "No one else was happy about it. They all want me to stay as the dark timekeeper. I don't know why! I'm not good at it. Barnabas thinks I can change things, but he used to be a light reaper. Nakita thinks it's a waste of time. Now the seraphs are mad at me. They think I'm not taking this seriously or that I don't understand what's at risk." Miserable, I wiped my eyes again and sniffed loudly.

"I'm happy," Josh said as he leaned forward.

At that, I let out a barking sound of a sob, dropping my head and letting go of his hands so I could wipe my face. "I'm tired of it all," I said, feeling it hit me hard as I admitted it aloud. "I'm tired of lying to my dad. Tired of fighting to make myself understood. Tired of not being able to sleep or eat. I just want to come home and be normal!"

I looked up at him through my wet eyes to see sympathy

but no understanding. "But," he started, and I shook my head, stopping him.

"Nakita is depressed because I might leave and forget about her. Barnabas is disappointed that I want to give up on something he's believed in for thousands of years but was too afraid to try for until now. I'm actually starting to figure things out, and somehow it's making things worse, not easier. I changed Tammy's aura today," I said, finding no joy in it. "And I stopped time. I stopped time, Josh! And I don't even care."

"Yes you do," he said, and I shook my head, but at least I was able to stop crying.

"For the first time," I said. "For the first time I feel like I can make a difference, but the seraphs won't give me a chance. I could do this timekeeper thing if they would just let me do it!"

Suddenly I realized how close we were. He had taken my hands again, and his knees, where they pressed against mine, were warm. He was listening to me, and it almost started me crying again. "I miss not being able to eat dinner with my dad," I whispered. "I miss waking up and looking at the sun on my wall and wondering what the day is going to be like."

I blinked, and a tear brimmed and fell. Josh wiped it away, and his hand taking mine again was damp.

"I miss being normal," I breathed, feeling drained and thinking about Paul, the rising light timekeeper. Sure, there was the icky factor of having Ron as a teacher, but he *did* have a teacher, and a life, and probably a girlfriend who didn't know he was someday going to be a friggin' timekeeper in charge of angels. He could pretend he was the same as everyone else. "Most time-keepers get to live their entire life before the old one dies and they have to set everything aside and be more than normal. I'm going to miss everything."

Okay, so maybe I was being a little drama queen, but Josh was the only person who I could tell this to who might understand.

"You're not going to miss everything," he said, and before I knew what he was doing, he leaned in and gave me a kiss.

A spark lifted in me. My hands tightened on his, and I shifted my head so our lips met more fully. My eyes closed, and I leaned in just a bit, feeling the space between us. Electricity spun down to my toes, and I pulled him closer.

It was awkward, sitting the way that we were, but it was the first time all day that I felt something other than confusion and desperation. I didn't want the kiss to end, but he slowly pulled back. The memory of my heartbeat thumped and my eyes opened. I felt breathless, though I knew I couldn't be. Josh was smiling, and his eyes flicked to mine and held, making me feel warm again.

"You want your body, right?" he asked, as if he hadn't just made every part of me come alive. I nodded, and he added, "So go get it."

I pulled back, worried. "You mean you think I should give

the amulet up?" I said, feeling a ping of alarm ring through me. "Just walk away from being the dark timekeeper?"

"No, of course not." He shifted, and our knees parted. "But Ron still has his body, right? He's alive and he's still the light timekeeper. So what's the big deal? You want it. Go get it. Being alive doesn't mean you have to give it up, does it?"

"No," I said hesitantly as I recalled my conversation with a seraph on that Greek island when I accepted the position. I had asked if I could take the amulet until I found my body, then return it, and the seraph had said I could if that was what I chose to do. If I chose now to have both, wouldn't that count for something?

Josh leaned in, surprising me when he kissed me again, lightly, almost teasingly as he took my fingers in his. "Just go get it. Let the rest figure itself out."

I looked at the hallway, thinking of my dad. "Now?"

Josh stood, grinning down at my reluctance. "Why not? If it had been me, I would have made Barnabas stop so I could have taken it when I first saw it. They live forever, Madison. What do they know? Go get your body, and I'll make you a sandwich. We can eat it and be normal. And when we're done being normal, we can call Barnabas and you can go back to saving the world. Jeez, Madison, even superheroes have real lives."

It was exactly what I wanted, what I'd been thinking about all day, and I sat at the table, unable to stop my fake heart from pounding. He made it sound so simple. I wanted it. To agonize over what everyone else thought I might do because I had my body was a stupid thing to do. "I'm going to do it," I said, and his smile grew wide.

"I knew you would." He gave me a soft smack on the shoulder. It wasn't as nice as that kiss, but I smiled back at him. Doing this felt right, for a change. Heaven be damned, if they didn't want to do things my way, then I'd just give the amulet back and to hell with them all.

Excitement zinged down to my toes, almost as potent as that kiss had been. I settled myself more firmly in the chair, setting it square to the table with my back to the hallway arch.

Josh made a sound of surprise. "Here? What if your dad comes in?"

He had moved to stand beside the coffeepot, concern in his expression, and I put my hand out, hoping he'd come sit beside me. "I want you with me when I do this," I said, my foot jiggling under the table. "You in my room after midnight isn't going to happen. Talk about my dad having a cow! The roof is out, too. Ron might still be out there."

"Okay, but we could go somewhere else," he said, arms crossing in front of him as he looked out the black window to the street.

"Barnabas is going to be here in an hour," I said impatiently. "There's nothing open. It will be fine, Josh. The first time I did this, I was in a cop's office. Besides, what do you think is going to happen? I slip into my body, and it's done!"

He made a face, and I wiggled my fingers at him, my palm up. "A kiss for luck?" I said, feeling myself grow warm. I couldn't wait to get my real body back. Everything I felt with Josh was being filtered through my amulet, and I just wanted to be myself again.

Josh chuckled at that, his arms uncrossing as he took the few steps that separated us. "A kiss for luck," he said, one hand taking mine, and the other going flat on the table between us. With a last look at the empty hallway as if my dad might be coming, he leaned over the table, tilted his head, and met my lips.

I breathed him in, imagining I could feel his aura swirling through mine. My eyes shut, and I leaned forward, our lips moving against each other as the memory of my heart gave a pound. *I want to be alive again,* I thought as my fingers tightened on his, and then let go.

His eyes opened as we pulled away, his gaze going to the hallway before they came back to me. "If you're sure?" he said, pulling out the chair facing the archway and sitting down.

My heart was still pounding, and I shrugged, licking my lips as if trying to seal the memory of him there. "Tell me if you hear him coming down, okay?"

Josh put his arms flat on the table, his head shaking. "Okay."

God, I hope this works. I felt like I was running out of time.

Smiling at Josh, I closed my eyes and resettled myself. I felt him take my hand, and I gave his fingers a squeeze. It was easy to find my mindscape of the sheet of the present and the tightly interwoven threads of everyone's lives falling from it. I could see Josh's blue twining heavily about mine, Barnabas and Nakita close in thought but not presence. Inching my awareness higher, I found the lines of my thought that were attaching to my amulet and pulling me into the future. And between them was the soft blue and yellow glow of my body, stuck in time, waiting for me.

"I can do this," I breathed as I let my awareness fall into the spaces in between.

Like a foot into a well-designed shoe, my soul gave a sigh and slipped into my body. The memory of Josh's lips on mine was replaced by the taste of salt. The hum of the fridge ebbed, and became the sound of surf. I gasped when a wrench twisted my gut.

Josh cried out, but it sounded thin and unreal. And with that same sort of mental relaxation I'd used to let go of the time line and get it started again, I let my mind slip back an instant in time. I hadn't before, and it made all the difference. With a little thunk of presence, I felt my body shift back in sync with the universe. I was here, and there was no going back.

My heart pounded, and a thrilling sensation spilled through me as I sat up in a spacious, sunlit room. I looked down at my torn prom dress, unbelieving as I felt the grimy fabric between two blood-caked fingers. That fast, it was done. I was in my body.

Dizziness hit me, and I took a gasping breath, almost forgetting to let it out. A laugh burbled up, mixing with the sounds of gulls. I had to breathe. I had to breathe!

My hand went to my neck, and I found my amulet. Swinging my feet around, I jerked my toes from the cold marble floor. Everything seemed to be moving slowly, and I ached everywhere. There was no toe tag when I looked, but I remembered having torn that off.

A throbbing at the front of my head brought my hand up, and I probed my forehead carefully, feeling what was probably a bruise. My shoulder and chest hurt. I pulled the dirt-stained, grimy dress from me to look down my front and see a long bruise where the seat belt would have been. I was really in my body. It was mine!

"I did it!" I shouted, hearing my voice echo, and the gulls outside seemed to mock me. Coughing, I hunched on the velveteen couch, holding my ribs so it wouldn't hurt so much.

"I did it," I whispered, not caring if I hurt. I had done it, and I wondered if my resonance had changed because I was again in my body. Black wings, I realized, wouldn't be a problem anymore. But then my victorious smile hesitated and slowly vanished. Moving carefully until I was sure I could, I stood up and hobbled toward the nearest door, frantically searching for the one thing I hadn't needed in six months. I had really done it. The proof, they say, is in the pudding. Or in this case, the can. I had to go to the bathroom in the worst way, and I didn't have a clue where it was.

EIGHT

I trailed my hand across the smooth marble walls just so I could feel the silky sensation as I left the bathroom. It had taken me an entire, desperate three minutes to find it. The huge washroom had been off an entire suite of rooms that I was guessing had been Kairos's private quarters. Kairos, the same guy who had killed me. I'd give the man one thing; he had taste. Everything I'd found in my mad dash for the bathroom had been scrumptiously elegant. Cold and precise. A band poster or CD rack would look out of place, which made me wonder how much time he'd actually spent here.

Giving the huge, sunken tub a last, longing glance from over my shoulder, I padded barefoot into the bedroom with its huge bed of soft pillows and downy comforters, still messed up from when Kairos had left it. Which was kind of creepy, when you thought about it. My body had been here all along, just an instant out of step with the rest of the world and therefore unseen and protected from the passage of time. Sort of like Barnabas hiding his wings, out of sync with the universe and invisible.

The sun coming in the huge windows with the flat ocean beyond it made me sigh. Taking a bath didn't sound prudent, even if I would feel a hundred percent better. I had changed clothes, though. Spending the rest of the night trying to save Tammy in my old prom dress wasn't an option. Kairos predictably hadn't had any skirts or dresses in his closet, but I'd found a black pair of trousers that almost fit if I rolled up the bottoms, and a baggy tunic that might be fashionable if you were in Azeroth in World of Warcraft.

I hoisted the baggy pants up higher and tied a small knot in the waistband to keep them from falling down as I went into the hallway. The shirt I couldn't do much with, and I'd just have to be careful not to lean too far forward. My old dress was wadded up and shoved under the bathroom sink. If I never saw it again, it would be too soon. Though caught in time and basically static for the time I'd been out of my body, I couldn't help but feel like I'd been wearing it since I'd died. No wonder my chest hurt, scrunched into that corset. My shoulder ached from the car accident, and I swung it experimentally, smiling. Yeah, it hurt, but it was because I was alive. I couldn't wait to tell Josh.

The hallway opened up into a huge common area with

fabulous cushions and low tables, which in turn led out to the spacious, tiled patio through wide archways edged in flowing curtains. I knew no one had been here since Kairos had died, but everything looked clean. One of the perks of living on holy ground, maybe?

I headed for the outside, my hand holding my amulet in reassurance. I was *so-o-o-o* glad I still had it and it hadn't been left behind in the kitchen when I had vanished, and I was sure I had. Barnabas had told me I had looked like a ghost when he yanked me back the first time, and since my amulet was what gave me my fake body, and it was with me now . . .

Poor Josh, I thought, wishing I had a way to talk soundlessly with him as I went outside and blinked in the sudden sun. He must be worried sick, me vanishing like that. As soon as I got myself thinking straight, I was going to contact Barnabas or Nakita to come pick me up. Nakita, at least, knew where Kairos's island was, seeing as she killed him here.

My eyes darted to the broken table where she'd scythed him, the cracked table empty of any sign of violence. I'd taken on the duties of the dark timekeeper before the blood of the last one had gone cold, and I shivered. The hard stone had been cracked when the seraph had laughed at me for not believing in fate. Or had it been laughing because it had seen the future and knew that I'd be here now, wanting my body and the amulet both. They'd let me keep it, right?

Concerned, I wrapped my arms around myself and turned

from the table as I remembered the painful beauty of the seraph. They'd let me keep the amulet. I mean, I'd asked if I could try it out, then give it back, and the angel had given me this crafty look and said I could if that was what I chose, like choice was all that there was when it was obvious that seraphs were all about fate. It had even said that there was always a choice. Well, I was making one now. Ron had an amulet, and he was alive. It had said I could choose to give up my amulet when I found my body. That meant the default was for me to keep it. Right?

Determination filled me, and the wind from the water rose up the hundred-foot drop from the tiny beach to shift my hair. The white cloth strung between the pillars made Kairos's patio look like a perfume commercial. The tide was mostly out, and I closed my eyes and faced the sun, hands spread wide as if I could take the moment and remember it forever, filling myself with the heat of the sun. My heart beat in my chest, and I breathed in and out. I was alive and it felt wonderful—even if my neck hurt as if I had whiplash.

Slowly my smile faded, and my head dropped. Somewhere, on the other side of the earth, Nakita waited in the darkness, thinking I was going to give up my position and abandon her. Some might think it unhealthy to have pinned so much on another person, but Nakita was an angel, one of heaven's finest reapers. For a creature who had existed since time began, fear was a world-altering realization. Her mind wasn't created to understand it, and I was her only way to figure it out. *Friend* was too simple a word. *Master* was just wrong. *Mentor* didn't fit. I only knew we had a bond, and I couldn't dismiss it just to make my life easier.

My hand gripping my amulet, I closed my eyes, thinking of Nakita's aura. Shifting my own aura so my thought could slip free of me, I sent a call to her, imagining her in my mind.

Nakita, I thought, feeling my emotion wing from me, and I modified it to her aura, exactly and precisely, right before it hit the top of the atmosphere and bounced down. Even if she were on the opposite side of the earth, she would hear.

But my thoughts stayed empty.

Frowning, I tightened my hold on my amulet. *Nakita!* I thought louder, taking more care to tailor it to her. Again it bounced from the ceiling of air back to earth . . . and simply vanished.

Concerned, I opened my eyes. I might be in some trouble here. Eventually they'd talk to Josh and figure out what I'd done, and since I had told Barnabas that I'd found my body on my island, they'd look for me here. How long that would take I didn't know. What might happen to Tammy in the meantime was not pretty.

Barnabas? I called, modifying my thought to slip past his aura and into his mind. I had always been able to reach him the easiest.

"Oh, crap," I whispered when I got the same response— which was no response. What the devil was going on? It was entirely possible that I'd accidentally changed my signature when I took my body, even if it looked the same to me. They might be hearing me and be unable to answer back. But I didn't think so. It was as if my thoughts weren't reaching them at all!

I spun to look at the broken table, fear making my stomach hurt. Maybe the seraphs had cut me off. They had been taking care of the dark timekeeper's duties for months. What if they had seen me take my body and they just cut me completely out of the equation and left me here before I could tell them I had made a new choice!

Clutching my amulet, I searched its depths. It looked the same, and scared, I stood with the drop-off to my back, the wind shifting my hair as I held my amulet and brought the time line into focus. It looked the same, too, and I exhaled in relief. My amulet, at least, worked.

"There once was a girl who was dead," Grace sang, and my eyes flew open as I spun, looking for her. "Whose decisions she made with her head. Her body to save, was just what she craved. Choice or fate—both were messed up, instead."

"Grace!" I exclaimed, hardly able to hear her over the loud surf, and squinting, still not seeing her glow in the bright sun. "I'm so glad you're here. Barnabas and Nakita . . . are they okay? I tried calling them, and they didn't answer. I'm still the dark timekeeper. Right?"

A faint buzzing tipped me off that she was nearby, and a warmth stole into my aching shoulder, soothing it. "Yup. You're still the dark timekeeper. They can't just take that away. You have to voluntarily give it up. Or be scythed."

My chest felt warm, and I wondered if she had moved to hover before me. "Your aura looks the same," she said, her voice going more faint. "Maybe they're just ignoring you. You smell funny now."

"Gee, thanks," I said, fully aware that I stank like I hadn't bathed in a month. There was nothing funny about it. "Do you think you could have one of them come get me? I'm worried about Tammy."

"You should be worried about Demus," she said cryptically.

"Demus?" I echoed, wondering what the dark reaper had done, but there was no answer. She was gone. I hadn't even seen her leave.

My brow furrowed, and I crossed my arms over my middle, feeing how empty it was. The elation at having gotten my body back was starting to fade. I was hungry, tired, and I ached from the injuries I'd gotten rolling down a hill in a convertible. It was starting to get hot, and my clothes fit funny. Looking at my nails and the old polish from the prom, I wished I had asked Grace to have Barnabas bring Josh with him. God, he must be worried sick.

The hair on the back of my neck seemed to prick, and I spun, heart pounding. There was no one there, just the big empty house that now belonged to me.

"Madison!" came from above, and I looked up, almost

blinding myself. It was Nakita, and I backed up under the canopy as she landed, her beautiful wings glinting in the afternoon sun. She was wearing all white again from her head to her boots, and I felt a pang of guilt. She only wore white when she was upset with me, her way of expressing her anger.

Her face was creased, but upon seeing me in my new black clothes pulled from Kairos's closet, confusion trickled into her eyes. "You're wearing Kairos's clothes," she said.

"I . . ." I said, then hesitated. "Well, I've got his job, right?" I said, sounding harsher than I intended. "I may as well do it right."

Nakita's lips parted, and her wings rose to block out the sun. "Then you're staying?"

"I don't know," I admitted, and her expression fell as if I'd told her I was leaving this moment. "Nakita, I'm trying, but nothing seems to be working," I pleaded with her. "You can see it better than I can. I don't want to think about it, okay? I just want to do right by Tammy. Then, when it's over, we can think about what comes next."

She seemed to accept that, her head down and the wind shifting her long black hair into her face. "I'm sorry the seraphs aren't listening to you," she said. "Barnabas found Demus. He went to find you, and found Josh instead. They are both waiting for you in the graveyard."

"Josh!" I exclaimed, glad he was going to be there.

"You need to talk to Demus," Nakita said tightly, "or he's

going to kill Tammy the second he sees her."

A faint smile came over me. "And that would be wrong, huh?" I asked her, and she blinked at me. Slowly her smile grew, and she looked almost embarrassed.

"It might be," she admitted, stretching her wings to put us both in the shade. "If there is a chance we can change her fate. We should go. I had forgotten how peaceful it is here." Her eyes met mine, holding not peace but at least a lack of fear. "Or maybe I never noticed before."

Nodding, I hoisted my pants back up and minced across the black marble to her. Nakita's arm went around me, and I stepped up on one of her feet, standing next to her, rather than in front. One push of her huge wings, and we were airborne. My stomach dropped, and I clutched at Nakita's arm. Looking down at the small island, I shivered. Flying was a lot scarier now that I was alive again.

"Close your eyes," Nakita warned me, and I screwed them shut. The muffling softness of her wings pressed against my ears as she enfolded us, and the scent of feathers and wind filled my nose. I gasped when the world seemed to turn inside out, but I was expecting it. Nakita had flung us across space, moving us from high noon to nearly midnight in an eyeblink.

A warm breeze shifted my hair, and I opened my eyes just as Nakita unfolded her wings and we dropped into space. Below us were the scattered lights of Baxter. Descending in a slow spiral, Nakita angled to a very dark part of town. It was the graveyard. A fitting spot, I thought, for a dark timekeeper to meet with her reapers.

"A reaper, Nakita, once saw, death comes to the big and the small," came Grace's faint voice, but I still couldn't see her. "Alone she once stood, thinking no one else would, but the truth empowers us all."

"Hi, Grace," I said, putting a hand to my stomach as we descended in the humid blackness. Man, we were a long way up. And the ground looked really hard.

"I'm not going to drop you," Nakita said as if she could read my thoughts, but it was probably my grip on her arm that gave me away.

I stumbled as she made the last wing-flapping movements in the air and my feet finally touched earth. My oversize shirt was slipping, and I yanked it back into place, warming as everyone looked up. Barnabas looked uneasy, clearly having guessed I had my body back, but Josh, standing beside him, grinned. Demus was leaning indolently against a large stone, his arms over his chest and his expression cross until he noticed what I was wearing, upon which he straightened to attention as if my clothes gave me status. Nakita had hidden her wings and was moving to stand hesitantly beside Barnabas. Grace, I'm sure, was somewhere about, but she wasn't moving, so who knew where her bright glow was.

"Hi, Josh," I said, and he ducked his head as he came forward, giving me a quick hug.

"You feel the same as before," he said, smiling with half his mouth as he gave me a squeeze.

"Thanks," I said, meaning for about six different things.

Barnabas cleared his throat, and Josh stepped back. "You scared the life out of me when you just vanished like that," Josh accused, then added proudly, "I knew you could do it. Some warning would have been nice."

"Sorry," I said, fidgeting as I turned to Barnabas.

"Congratulations," Barnabas said as he handed me my phone, his tone not giving me a clue as to what he thought about me getting my body back, and my smile started to fade.

"Yes, well, nothing has changed," I said as I fumbled for a place to stash it before I handed it to Nakita to put in her purse. "Except I'm hungry."

Demus pushed himself from the tombstone, squinting as he approached. "You're wearing Kairos's clothes and his amulet, but you don't look anything like him."

"And we're all glad of that," Nakita said, earning a chime of laughter from Grace, who was hiding somewhere.

"There was a cross-dresser from France," she started, and Nakita threw a rock at her. It went clattering into the dark, and I swear I heard a cat yowl.

I looked down at my clothes. The reapers seemed to be making more out of me wearing them than I'd intended. "I, uh, was in that old prom dress. It was kind of icky. This was the only thing that remotely fit."

"You look fine," Barnabas said, but his eyes were on the dark school behind me.

"Well, I think you still smell funny," Grace whispered right next to my ear, and I jumped.

"Grace, flap your wings a little," I said. "It's eerie not knowing where you are!"

I was just in time to see the worried look exchanged between Nakita and Barnabas. "You can't see her?" Barnabas asked, and I flushed again. Man, I was starting to miss being dead.

"I've never been able to see her very well. It's dark out here," I said, wondering if I was seeing the tip of my new iceberg. First I wasn't able to contact Nakita or Barnabas, and now I was having a hard time seeing Grace. It didn't help that Nakita was still looking at Barnabas like I was broken.

My stomach growled, and I levered myself up to sit on the nearest tombstone. "Okay, the seraphs are mad," I said.

"Understatement," Demus said bluntly as he tossed his amulet up and caught it.

"They sent you to scythe her," I added, making sure we all knew where we stood.

"The moment I find her," Demus said, throwing his amulet up again into the inky black.

Barnabas reached out, and the dark stone smacked into his hand. Demus sat up fast. "I won't let you kill her," Barnabas said. "She might be able to keep her soul alive, rekindle it. You don't know."

"They never do!" Demus shouted, lunging. Barnabas side-stepped him, smacking his butt with the flat of his sword, brought into existence in the time it takes for an electron to spin. Josh grabbed my elbow, and I slid from the stone, putting it between us and the reapers.

Demus caught his balance, his face twisted into an ugly snarl. "I will kill her," he vowed. "I will save her soul from butchers like you, breaking seraph will. Choice is *nothing* compared to fate. *Nothing!* Or you'd be able to change it, and you can't! Give me back my amulet!"

My eyes were wide, and I gripped the stone I was standing behind, Josh firmly next to me. Barnabas had taken the stone to keep Demus from having the ability to kill Tammy, but that wasn't how I wanted to change things, and I gave a directive head-toss in Demus's direction.

Barnabas's lips pressed together disapprovingly, but he lobbed it back to the angry angel even as Nakita scoffed. "But we have changed fate, dark reaper," Barnabas said as Demus caught it. "The seraphs just don't want you to know about it."

"If the seraphs don't tell me, then I don't need to know," Demus said, cradling his amulet as he hunched protectively over it. "Soon as I find her, I take her soul to save it," Demus said, then turned to Nakita. "Why are you even listening to this? Are you going grim, Nakita?"

Nakita stiffened, her features lost in the dark as she crossed her arms over her middle. Nakita wasn't grim, but I could see why he asked.

"You can't find her because I changed Tammy's resonance," I said, my bare feet going damp in the grass as I came from around the stone and walked toward him. "And you are not going to kill Tammy. You, dark reaper, are going to help me find her, and then we are *not* going to scythe her. We are going to talk to her and show her a different choice so she stirs her soul back to life before it dies completely. That's how we do things down here now. Barnabas saved someone ages ago. And we saved someone else just last month. It can be done."

"Life is transitory. Souls are not to be risked," he said, backing away.

"If her soul is to be lost, then we will save it, but not at the cost of her life!" I said, then lowered my voice before someone called the cops about voices in the graveyard. "I *am* the dark timekeeper," I said, pushing forward until his back found a tombstone. "I survived my predecessor killing me. I survived black wings eating me alive. I am *going* to change things," I said, my heart pounding. "And you are going to help me. Got it?"

He didn't say yes. But he didn't say no, either. "Who am I?" I insisted.

"You're the dark timekeeper," he muttered, his expression going from defiance to one of a sullen understanding. "Nakita, this is stupid. Haven't you told her that you can't change fate?"

"Of course I did." Nakita, who had been doing handstands

against a tombstone, walked on her palms toward us. Flipping right side up, she landed in a fighting pose. "And then she proved me wrong. We saved Ace."

"Barnabas . . ." Demus almost whined.

The angel smiled with half his mouth, still leaning on his sword. "Just go with it," he advised. "But if you try to scythe Tammy, I *will* stop you."

Demus crossed his arms over his chest, defiant, but understanding. "Why not just let Ron put a flipping guardian angel on her and be done with it?" he said belligerently. "If you want to save someone's life, that's how you do it."

"Because we're not just trying to save her life, we're trying to save her soul *and* her life," I said, not knowing how to explain it to him. It was about free will and choice, and angels just didn't get it. Like Barnabas had said, heaven was black and white, but the earth was colorful.

Slumping to the ground, Demus sat cross-legged. "Sweet seraph toes, I don't get it."

His head shaking at the angel's confusion, Josh gingerly sat on a broken stone. "Intense, and a little dense, too," he whispered to me, and I smiled.

Barnabas put his sword away, clearly relaxing as Demus backed off. "So how do we talk to her?" he asked, then added, "Without her calling the cops on you. I mean, she does think you started the fire, right? Do you want me to wipe her memory?"

"No," I said quickly, head down as I began to pace in the wet grass. "That's why marks don't change. You take their memories, and they have nothing to make a change with." I came to a halt and pulled my head up. "Everyone leaves Tammy's memories alone. Got it?"

Demus groaned, rocking back as he sat there cross-legged. "This is the weirdest scything I've ever been on."

I couldn't help my smile. "That's because it's not a scything, it's a rescue."

His head thrown back to the stars, Demus moaned, "This isn't going to work."

My stomach growled, and I turned to the empty street. "I'm sure Tammy would appreciate us trying." And he was wrong. It would work. It had to.

"Never going to wo-o-o-ork," Demus sang, and Nakita threw a rock at him.

"Shut up!" she exclaimed as Demus ducked and the rock shattered into fragments on the stone behind him. "She's the dark timekeeper and you're going to listen!"

"It's okay, Nakita," I said as I felt the sudden adrenaline rush banish my tiredness. "He sounds like you used to. He'll learn."

Barnabas ran a hand through his curls, his eyes on my bare toes. "There's only one problem," he said, giving Nakita a worried glance.

"And that would be . . . ?" I prompted, thinking it likely wasn't my lack of shoes.

"Your amulet," he said, his gaze flicking to it and back to me. "I don't think it's working."

"What do you mean?" I said, grasping it like it might vanish.

Barnabas shrugged. "What I mean is that Grace has been talking to you for the last five minutes, and you haven't heard a word she's said."

NINE

"No!" I exclaimed, my grip on my amulet becoming tighter as Josh straightened, concern pinching his brow. "I could hear her before!" Barely, though, and I hadn't seen her at all. "And I can see the time lines!" I added, bringing them up in my thoughts.

But panic iced through me, and I stared at Barnabas. All I could see in my mindscape was a hazy glow, like the imprint a bright light might leave on your retina. "It's almost not there!" I yelped. "They cut me off. The seraphs cut me off. No wonder I couldn't reach either of you earlier. Try to talk to me, Barnabas. Talk to me!"

Barnabas gave me a pained look. "I've tried. Been trying. Madison, I don't think you've been cut off."

"Then my aura has shifted." I was babbling, but I couldn't help it. Josh had risen, but I was frantic, and I wouldn't let him touch me when he tried to put a hand on my shoulder.

"We can see that, and compensate," Nakita said. She was standing next to Barnabas. I think it was the first time they had ever made a united front.

Demus flopped back against the grass and stared up at the stars, completely uncaring. "Like a light reaper can hear a dark timekeeper," he scoffed.

"They can," Josh said belligerently.

"And I'm not light," Barnabas added, his angry tone shocking me out of my own fear. I stared at him, and his gaze dropped as if he was ashamed. "Not anymore."

My lips parted, making my fear hesitate. He had admitted it. Barnabas had let go of the last of himself. His eyes were on my amulet, and I took my hands off it, letting it dangle freely. "If they haven't cut me off, then I broke it when I took my body," I said. "Damn it, how long do you think before it fixes itself?"

Nakita was waving her hand in front of her face, backing up. "I will!" she was saying to Grace, probably, since I didn't think Nakita was psychotic. "Just shut up a moment, okay?" Exhaling, she turned to me. "Grace says that your amulet is fine."

I looked at Josh, almost wishing I'd never taken my body back, and he dropped his eyes. It wasn't his fault. I made the choice. "Then they cut me off—" I started.

"No," Nakita insisted. "Madison, will you just listen? They didn't cut you off, and you didn't break it by claiming your body. But you're alive now, and that's a problem."

My swirling thoughts slowed. "Why is that a problem?" I asked.

Barnabas, though, was nodding his head. "Remember when you first flashed forward into Ace's future and it was too much for you?" he said, and I took Josh's hand, giving it a quick squeeze at the memory of stars so beautiful they almost broke me. "You were dead," he said. "Halfway to the divine. Ron had to adjust your amulet for you? It's still toned down, and now that you're alive, you're not making a strong enough connection."

"Oh, ma-a-a-an," I groaned, dropping back to slump against a tall tombstone. Muffled. Everything was muffled. "You think?" I asked, my voice quavering. If that was all it was, it could be fixed. Not by me, though. Ron had fixed it the last time.

"You should have waited and gotten your body back *after* we saved Tammy," Barnabas said.

I gave Barnabas a dark look, relieved that it wasn't anything that the seraphs did to curtail me. Grace *had* said something about how my decision to claim my body messed up both fate and chance. I'd just have to deal with it. *How am I going to deal with it?*

"So we look for her on foot," Josh said, seeming as relieved as I was. "What's the big deal? We have enough people. We should hit the bus depots and all-night places first. There isn't much open. How hard can it be?"

"You'd be surprised," Demus said to the stars. "Finding someone on foot isn't as easy as it sounds."

Nakita nudged him with the toe of her white boot. "Saving a mark isn't easy, reaper. It's hard work. Get used to it."

Scowling, he swung at her foot, and she danced back, laughing at him, enjoying herself.

Barnabas was frowning—as usual. "Finding her visually will take too long. Even if we split up. This would be a lot easier if you hadn't changed her resonance," he grumbled.

"Maybe you can ask the seraphs to fix your amulet," Josh said, sitting back down on his broken grave marker.

"Yeah, like they would do that now?" Demus said with a harsh laugh. "Madison, they are so mad at you."

"Ron maybe?" Nakita offered, looking like she had swallowed something nasty, and I shook my head.

"He doesn't know we're here," Barnabas said. "I think we should keep it that way."

He probably suspected we were here, but *I* wasn't going to bring it up. Not being able to see the time line was going to be a problem. I knew what Tammy's resonance looked like now, but I couldn't show anyone if the time line was a blurred mess to me. I didn't think reapers could backtrack by themselves into the past to see where her aura shifted unless I was there to guide them. It would take a timekeeper for that. Or perhaps . . . one studying to be a timekeeper?

Elated, I yanked my borrowed pants back up. "Paul," I said

firmly, and everyone stared.

"Paul?" Nakita echoed, disbelief in the slant of her eyes.

"Who's Paul?" Josh whispered.

Demus had sat back up to better laugh at me. "You mean the rising light timekeeper?" he snorted, and Josh's expression darkened. Yeah, he remembered him now.

"Paul isn't skilled enough to tweak your amulet," was Barnabas's opinion, but I was waving at them to listen.

"Yeah, I know. But he can help us find Tammy. He can look at the time line back to where I changed her aura. He can show both of you." I glanced at Demus. "The three of you, I mean. And once you have that. Ba-da-bing! We have her."

Demus was eyeing me in disbelief. "Uh, we're talking Ron's grub, right?"

Grub? I thought. How insulting is that?

Nakita had crossed her arms in front of her, looking immovable. "This is not a good idea. Even for you, Madison." Josh, too, had turned away and was scuffing the turf with the toe of his boot. He wasn't jealous, was he? I wondered, feeling a flash of delight.

"Why not?" I asked, not caring that everyone thought it was a bad idea. When had I ever had an idea they thought was good? "Paul helped us before. We never could have saved Ace if it wasn't for his help."

The words were out of my mouth before I had a chance to

think about them, but it was true. Dark and light working together had done it.

"Oh, come on!" I almost moaned as Nakita rolled her eyes. "You got any better ideas?"

Barnabas gave up with a long exhale. "If she wants to try it, why not?" he said, and Nakita's lips parted in surprise.

"Great," Demus said as he stood and stretched. "You go talk to the rising light timekeeper, and I'll go check in with the seraphs."

Barnabas spun, his long coat unfurling. His hand was on his amulet, and his threat was obvious. "You show even one feather to leave, and I'll cut your wings off. You're Madison's reaper, and you'll do as she says, so help me God!"

"Gee, thanks, Barnabas," I said to try to lighten things up, and Demus slumped. Apparently Barnabas's swordsmanship was legendary.

"I guess I'm in, then," the dark reaper said.

I smiled at that. Demus wasn't really a bad guy. Just focused on old methods. Nakita had been, too, and she had been far more militant in voicing her opinion. Still smiling, I held out my hand to Nakita. "Can I have my phone?" I asked sweetly, and Demus made an odd, strangled sound.

"Sweet seraph nubs, she's going to phone him?" the reaper gasped, and Josh sighed, falling back to stand against a tall pillar with his arms over his middle. He was starting to look cold.

I knew I was. *And he's jealous!*

I smiled my thanks as Nakita handed me my little pink phone, the battery charged and five bars showing. Magic, technology . . . it was pretty much the same thing to me. The important thing was that we were going to do this together. I couldn't do it alone. I didn't think it was even possible to do alone. It was going to take all of us. Light and dark.

"She has his number?" Demus asked in disbelief as I went through my phone book and hit ICE.

"When did you get his number?" Josh asked, his voice clipped.

"Last month," I said, listening to it ring. "I got it from Shoe, and thought it would be a good idea." Josh was still staring at me, and I made a questioning face. "What's the big deal here? I'm a timekeeper, he's trying to be one. I've got him as my emergency number in case, I don't know . . . I get put in jail for starting a fire or something."

Josh turned away, and faintly, almost at the edges of my hearing, I thought I heard Grace huff and say that she was all the protection I'd ever need.

"Am I the only one who sees a problem in this?" Demus was saying. "Nakita, she's betraying everything the seraphs believe in. Everything *we* believe in."

"Shut up and watch," Nakita shot back at him, but I could tell she was worried.

The phone was still ringing, and I fidgeted with it to my ear, wondering if the warmth I felt on my face was from Grace.

"'Ello?" a tired voice came on, and my tension doubled.

"Paul, it's Madison," I said, and Paul said nothing. "Dark timekeeper?" I prompted, then felt a flush of worry. Maybe I'd gotten the number wrong. "Crap, is this Paul?"

"Oh! Hi, Mark," Paul said, and I froze until I realized he wasn't alone. "Sorry, I fell asleep on the couch watching a movie. Sure. Hold on and I'll get it. It's in my lab book. You've got all weekend to do it. Couldn't you have called tomorrow?"

Demus was leaning against a rock again, his disgust obvious. "He doesn't even know who you are."

"Relax," Barnabas said, leaning close to whisper it. "He's with Ron is all. That's the problem with you dark reapers. You don't know how to lie properly."

Demus's expression became irate, but I thought it was funny.

There was a smattering of background noise, the sound of a door closing, and then Paul's hushed voice saying, "Are you insane? Why are you calling me?"

"Why did you tell me I could if you didn't want me to?" I asked him.

"It was in case of an emergency!" Paul said, then hesitated. "What did you do?"

I would have taken offense, but I *had* kind of screwed up. "Um, I found my body. And now my amulet doesn't work right."

"Congratulations?" he said, making it into a question.

"See?" Nakita said, leaning forward so she could hear. "Even the grub knows it was a mistake."

"It wasn't a mistake!" I said, but I was starting to think that it was. Giving her a dark look, I turned back to the phone, my eyes on Josh's. He looked mad, or maybe worried. "Paul, I need your help," I said. *Jeez, I hope he hadn't heard the grub comment.*

He sighed. I heard it even though he was probably several hundred miles away in an Arizona desert. "Are you trying to change someone's fate again?" he asked. "Madison, it was luck the last time. Fate is fate. That's why they call it that."

"I thought you believed in choice?" I mocked him, then caught my anger, swallowing it. Paul didn't say anything, and my worry crept back. "Paul?"

"For God's sake," he said, voice hushed. "Do you know what Ron will do to me if he finds out I helped you?"

My hand holding the phone to my ear trembled. "Her name is Tammy," I said. "Her soul was going to start to die after her brother died in a fire. I talked to her, and her fate changed so they both died, so I talked to them again, and something shifted so that they survived. She listened, Paul, and I reminded her of the good stuff. She wants to change, but she's not out of it yet. She's still in danger of letting her soul die. I need to find her. Talk to her again. I know I can fix this."

Demus was peering at me in question. His eyes met mine and held. "This is a big mistake," he said, his voice utterly devoid of the devil-may-care attitude he had shown so far.

166

"She still isn't making the choice to live," I said to Paul, but talking to both of them. "But I think she can. I changed her resonance to hide her from the reapers and I can't find her because my amulet . . ." I took a breath. "Paul, my amulet is tuned to a dead person, not one halfway to heaven." *Or hell.* "I can't find her. Please, just help me find her, and then you can go back to your movie or whatever you were doing. Five minutes, tops."

"You changed her resonance?" Paul asked, a hint of jealousy in his voice.

"Yes," I said, feeling a stirring of pride. My eyes flicked to Josh again. He still wasn't looking at me, and I felt a ping of anger. Save me from the touchy male ego. "Help me find Tammy, and I'll tell you how I did it."

"You can't teach the rising light timekeeper!" Demus exclaimed, and Barnabas shoved him over.

"I can't see the time lines," I admitted, starting to get nervous. "Paul, we have to find her before the light reaper does and puts a guardian angel on her."

Again he sighed. "Or I could sit here and do nothing, and Tammy's life is saved by a guardian angel," Paul finally said.

"A guardian angel doesn't save anything," I said in frustration, working to keep the irritation from my voice because I *was* trying to gain his help. "It just means that her life goes on. No meaning, Paul. No grace. She may as well be a painting on the wall. I'm not going to ask the seraphs for help. Grace says they're ticked at me, and I think it's because I'm proving them wrong and they don't like it."

It felt good to say it, and my face warmed even as I turned from the reapers watching me with varying degrees of hope and disbelief. Paul was silent again, but there was nothing more I could say, and I waited, fidgeting.

"Where are you?" he said flatly, and I took a huge breath of air, thrilled to my toes. Demus softly swore, and Barnabas and Nakita exchanged a high five. Josh smiled softly, and I warmed. "Puerto Rico?" he guessed. "Ron just sent someone out there."

"Baxter, California," I said, feeling like this might work even though he hadn't said yes yet. "I'm not sure where that is exactly. Somewhere south? It's hot and muggy."

Paul made a soft *mmmm* of sound. "I think I know where that is. Let me get my shoes. Ron was griping about one of the reapers not checking back in."

"Arariel," I said, and Paul made a grunt of acknowledgment.

"Yes, that's her. Hold on. I gotta tell Ron I'm going to bed."

Hold on? I wondered, but the phone made a high-pitched squeal. Yelping, I dropped it, scrambling to catch it and missing. "Sorry," I said after I picked it up and gingerly put it back to my ear. "Paul? Paul, you there?"

But Paul wasn't there anymore, and I spun at a bright light that lit the graveyard. Ten feet away, a vertical line split the darkness, widening until a black shadow grew at its center. It was Paul, closing his phone as he stepped from one part of the world to the other as easily as crossing into another room. His smile widened as his unlaced dress shoes found the dew-wet grass and the bright line behind him closed in on itself and vanished.

Nodding respectfully to Barnabas and Nakita, he let his gaze linger on Demus, who was eyeing him with mistrust, then blinked in surprise when Josh pushed himself up from the pillar, obviously the odd man out, not being a reaper.

"Hi, Madison," Paul said lightly as he tucked his dress shirt back in his Dockers, fully aware that I was as impressed as all hell. "Who are we saving tonight?"

TEN

Demus dropped back to take in Paul. "Your aura is green?" he mocked, staring at the luminescent stone around Paul's neck. The glow of the stone was a reflection of Paul's aura, and it was indeed a bright, gold-laced green.

Paul dropped his eyes, his lips set tight as he ran a hand over his sandy-brown hair. He was embarrassed, and I didn't think it was because he was still wearing the rumpled clothes that he'd worn to school today. The stone he used to touch the divine should be shifting up the spectrum to a light timekeeper's red by now, but it was that sparkly, neutral green, as Demus had so inelegantly pointed out, that ebbed to a flat black even as I watched.

"You shut up." Nakita threatened to smack him, and I cleared my throat. I thought it odd she was defending Paul, seeing as she didn't like him, but she *had* apologized to Paul for knocking him out once, so maybe it was part of her trying to understand. Barnabas, too, looked more uncomfortable now that Paul was here.

"You're not doing this!" Demus said, ignored, and I didn't like the look in his eye.

"I can't stay long," Paul said, glancing at everyone, his gaze lingering on Josh questioningly.

"The rising light timekeeper should not be here!" Demus hissed, and I jerked when I felt him tap into the divine. Barnabas was already moving, his dark shadow darting across the open area to slam into the redheaded angel.

"Look out!" Nakita shouted, and I found myself on the ground, the air pushed out of my lungs and Nakita on top of me. Damn, she was fast! Blowing the hair out of my eyes, I wiggled to get a better look as Barnabas sat on Demus, a handful of red hair in his grip as he pulled Demus's head up. Paul had fallen back, knowing to get out of the way when angels fought, and Josh was behind that pillar again.

Barnabas lifted the chain around Demus's neck until he had his amulet in his possession. "Nakita, do you have any rope in that purse of yours?"

"Get off me, Nakita," I wheezed. Yeah, my life was so glamorous, out after midnight among the tombstones, sweating and slapping at mosquitoes.

Nakita slipped off, and I took a huge gulp of air, sitting up to brush last week's dried grass clippings off me. Nice. I hadn't been in my new dark timekeeper clothes five minutes and I get them dirty. Josh extended a hand to help me up, and I took it gratefully.

"Thanks," I said softly, my lips next to his ear. "And relax, will you? You look like he wants to be my boyfriend or something. He's just a guy."

"Yeah?" Josh said as he watched me brush the last of the dirt off. "Just a guy who can do that amulet thing and walk through space."

I grinned at him, appreciating that he felt jealous. "He's not the one who held my hand when I died," I said, shifting my weight to bump into him. "And he's not the one who was there when I got my body back."

Josh's shoulders eased, and he actually smiled, even when Paul came to stand at my other side. The two guys warily greeted each other as Nakita leaned against a stone and pulled her long stockings off.

"This is wrong!" Demus was shouting, and I looked at the dark street that suddenly seemed too close. "The seraphs need to know what you're doing! That grub is going to tell Ron. He's going to put a guardian angel on her!"

I had broken curfew too many times and gotten away with it to be cowed by what a seraph might think about me hanging out with my future adversary. They were the ones who picked me. If they couldn't handle my rebellious tendencies, then they should have picked someone else. Still . . . I watched the sky. Demus couldn't do much without his amulet, but there was no need to advertise.

"Here," Nakita said as she handed Barnabas her white stockings. Barnabas tossed me the reaper's amulet, and I caught it, feeling the violet stone warm in my grip as both Paul and I looked down at it. I hadn't made it, but the amulet around my neck had been used in its construction, and it was as if the two stones were greeting each other.

"Get off!" Demus huffed as Barnabas yanked his arms back and tied his wrists. "Nakita," he pleaded when Barnabas finished and got off him. "He's going to put a guardian angel on her. Nakita, stop this! You're traitors! Traitors!" he shouted.

Feet spread wide, Nakita stood over him as Barnabas yanked him into a seated position. "I told you to be quiet," she said, bending provocatively to shove her last wadded-up stocking into his mouth. "And I'm not a traitor," she added, looking unsure as she stepped back.

Paul gave me a look like he wanted to laugh but was afraid to. "Having problems with your reapers?"

My heart was pounding. Demus's face was as red as his hair. "He's new to my methods," I said with a false lightness, then turned away as if it didn't bother me. But it did.

Paul grinned, reaching out a finger to poke my shoulder. "You're alive now?"

I couldn't help but smile back. "Yeah, so no scything me, okay?"

He laughed, pantomiming cutting through me with a blade, remembering our first meeting when he'd tried to kill me. I had been evil incarnate, according to him. Now I was hoping he saw us as colleagues . . . sort of. Glancing at Demus, Paul said, "I don't know exactly what you want me to do here."

Excitement tingled to my toes. "Your amulet is strong enough to see the time lines, right?" I asked. "I mean, Ron didn't give you an amulet that couldn't, yes?"

Paul looked down at his green stone. "I can see them, sure. But that doesn't help you much. I don't have the slightest idea where to look."

Barnabas gave Demus a nudge to be quiet. "What have you been doing the last three months?"

"Not this," was Paul's quick, defensive answer, and Josh snorted.

"If you can bring the time lines up," I said, "I can see them through your thoughts. I'll show you her resonance, like I would a reaper."

Paul's eyes were wide. "You can do that? Show someone else what you're looking at?"

"It's how a timekeeper shows a reaper what soul to take," I said, realizing that Ron hadn't told him that much. Sure, Paul could jump across space and make a sword from the divine, but he didn't know the first thing about his *job*. What was Ron waiting for?

"Like I said," Barnabas muttered as he leaned toward me, "what *have* you been doing the last three months?"

I glared at Barnabas to be quiet. We needed Paul's help. "You want to try it?" I asked Paul. If he didn't, we were screwed.

Paul glanced at Josh, then me. "You, uh, won't be able to read my thoughts, will you?" he asked.

I looked at Nakita and Barnabas, not sure myself, and they shrugged. Maybe this wasn't such a good idea. "I don't know. Paul, you're going to have to do this eventually," I cajoled, and his eyes grew determined.

"Okay," he said, sitting down on one of the stones.

Nakita made a tiny huff. Arms over her chest, she leaned toward Barnabas. "Why is it they both have to sit down to do stuff?"

Nervous, I sat across from Paul, feeling the damp go right through my thin clothes. I took three breaths, trying to center myself as Barnabas had taught me. It was a lot harder now that I was alive. I guessed that taking Paul's hand might improve the chances we could pull this off, but Josh was scowling again, and I didn't.

"Okay, I found it," Paul said, his expression calm as he looked at his inner mindscape. "I found you." His one eye cracked open as he compared my real aura with the one on the time line. "Found them," he added, meaning the reapers, I guessed as he glanced at them. Then he cringed. "Madison, I have no idea what I'm looking at."

"Hold on," I said. Closing my eyes, I brought up my mindscape. As I feared, there wasn't much to look at, just that blurry haze of nothing.

"Try touching him," Nakita said dryly, and Josh exhaled loudly.

"Okay," I said, then reached for him.

"Hey!" he yelped.

I got a flash of bright light, and then it was gone. My eyes flew open, and I stared at Paul. He looked scared, his eyes wide in the dim light of the distant streetlamp. My heart pounded, and I realized my hand was fisted in my lap. "Are you okay?" I asked him as Barnabas grumbled.

"Yeah," he said, clearly flustered. "It just surprised me. Let's try again."

Demus made some muffled comment that we all ignored, and Paul reached for my fingers. Nervous, I took his hand. It was smooth in mine, and a little sweaty. Or maybe the sweat was from me.

Nakita snorted, and I gave her a dark look before closing my eyes. Immediately I was struck by how fuzzy everything still was. It was like going from high-def to normal TV. Or maybe taking your glasses off. The exquisite definition of everyone's life lines was muted and blurry. It was still easy to tell, though, where Paul and I were. Nakita, Barnabas, and Demus were even easier to find, their glows twining around us almost protectively.

Here, I thought, not knowing if Paul could hear me, and I drifted my awareness down into the time lines until I found Tammy, not too far away, still alone, very alone, her new aura with the black-rimmed, orange center shining dully. Paul's bright glow was beside mine, and the reapers' auras, too. All we had to do now was find her in reality.

We can do this, I thought with a resurgence of hope. My fingers tightened in Paul's grip, and he squeezed back. But before I could even relax my hold and break our connection, the entire line flashed blue.

Holy crap! I thought, my grip tightening spasmodically. *It's a flash forward!*

In an instant, Paul and I were alone. The reapers were gone. I could feel Paul's confusion, then fear as he realized something was wrong. His fingers loosened in mine, and I gripped them tighter, frantically trying to keep him with me. If he let go, we'd lose it.

It's a flash forward! I thought, trying to maintain my grip on his fingers and my sight on the line. *I can't see if you leave!*

I had probably been trying to flash forward all night, but my connection had been too weak. Now, with Paul, it was enough. I was desperate to see Tammy's future, and it was with a huge sigh of relief that I felt Paul's confusion turn to excitement.

His fingers in mine wiggled, and around us, the line became a darker blue, almost black. With a curious flipping sensation, we were out of the present, and in . . .

Tammy, I thought, familiar with the sensation of being in someone else's mind, a silent observer as a myriad of moments flitted through someone else's consciousness. At least this time she wasn't in a burning apartment.

The softness of sheets was what I noticed first, then Paul's presence next to mine. His quicksilver thoughts were jumping from idea to idea, his excitement contagious. Knowing it wouldn't help, I willed Tammy to open her eyes. And she did.

The shock of that reverberated through me, and I took in the too-narrow, propped-up bed, the industrial-looking built-in counter and drawers, the blank TV fixed high to the wall, and the long, ugly table on wheels. There was an oversize cup on it, the straw bent away, and a single get-well card. The sun was up, but it wasn't coming in the open window that had a view of a brick wall. I couldn't tell if we were two stories up, or thirty. The hazy blue indicating a far-distant flash forward hung on the edges of my vision, and I realized Tammy was squinting as I struggled to get a clearer view.

When are we? I heard Paul ask, another surprise, but I didn't think Tammy heard since she didn't react.

I don't know. A few days from now? A week maybe? No more than that, I guessed.

And then a new thought intruded, clear and resolved. *I'm dying.*

My heart gave a jump, and I felt Paul's grip tighten in mine when Tammy moved her hand above the sheets. It was horribly thin, the skin pale and almost transparent, looking too weak to even tie a shoelace. A bruise was around her wrist where someone had gripped her, and her fingernails were painted a bright red, garish against the white sheets. An ache filled our entire body, as if in a fever, and I wondered if she had been beaten. The blue haze surrounding everything put it a few days ahead at most, but there was no way she could lose this much weight that fast, and I wondered why the vision was so clear. We must be months, maybe years ahead.

The breath labored in our chest, and I felt a tear slide down Tammy's cheek. Inside, I could feel her pulse becoming erratic, and a weird tingling rose up from her toes. She said she was dying. She might be right.

A feeling of worthlessness had filled our joined thoughts as the sound of traffic came in the open, small window set in the large pane of glass. She was alone, but that was not why she cried. Regret. Regret for words not said, for thoughts left unspoken, for actions not taken, and challenges not acknowledged. And only now, at the end, did she understand what she had lost by shutting out the good things and living her life without love. Even her brother, who she had turned away so often that he had quit trying.

Tammy, it's okay, I thought, trying to reach her. *It's not too late!*

But only Paul heard me.

My chest clenched in heartache as she thought of drawings she never began and poems stopped with only one phrase—afraid of what others would think. There were trips not taken and friends never joined, chances to make someone else happy that she ignored, thinking that it made her stronger, when all it did was eat away at her soul.

"I wish . . ." she breathed, her head turning to the window and the dismal brick wall. "I wish . . ."

But it was too late, and I felt a lump in my throat as a small glint of dust glittering in the corner took on the familiar glow. It was a guardian angel weeping sunbeams, and I wondered if this was why the far flash forward was so clear.

Paul started in surprise, and then I realized by Tammy's sudden exhalation of breath that she saw her, too. *Is that an angel?* he asked me, and I sent a sideways thought to him that it was. *Why is she crying?* both Tammy and he wanted to know.

"Because your life is over," the angel said aloud, her chiming voice like falling water both familiar and different from Grace's.

Tears slipped from me. From us. We were all the same. "You're so beautiful," Tammy breathed, clearly able to see her, too. "Have you come for me?"

The hope in her voice went to my core and twisted, and

hearing it, the angel dropped down before her, bathing her in warmth as the room seemed to go cold and dark.

"I've been with you since forever and no time at all," the angel said, smiling through her own tears.

"I know. I felt you," Tammy said. "I think I felt you. I'm so sorry," she said around a gulp of air, the tears spilling over and blurring our shared vision.

"What for, child?"

Her pale hand lifted and fell, looking unnatural as it lay palm up on white, faded sheets. "I ran away. I don't just mean from Johnny and my mother, but from everything. I had so many plans. I was going to do so many things, and I can't even remember them now."

She was dying, six thousand sunrises behind her, a billion emails sent, a thousand jokes laughed at, a zillion moments tucked in her brain to add up to nothing because she had forgotten how to love. She was still that same scared girl I had tried to help hours ago, frightened and thinking she was alone.

The angel dropped even lower, coming to rest in the cup of her hand. "You must be brave now," she admonished, crying, still crying.

A spike of fear lit through her and died. "Why?" she whispered.

"It's going to hurt."

The fear redoubled, and Tammy held her breath. *Why?* she thought, her question echoing in both Paul's and my minds.

"I won't leave you. I'll stay until it's over," the angel said like a parent reassuring a child they wouldn't leave until he fell asleep, and the warmth of her stole up Tammy's arm and settled in her chest.

Am I going to die? Tammy asked, her thought quavering.

"You've already done that, love."

Fear, my own this time, filled me. It was true. Tammy was dead. She had not taken another breath since the angel had told her it was going to hurt. I felt Paul's panic, and I squished my own terror. We were okay. We weren't dead. *But Tammy was.*

What's going to happen to me? Tammy asked, her thoughts clearer now among ours.

And still the angel cried. "I'm sorry," she said, beautiful in her sorrow. "I wish I could make it different, but all I'm made for is to protect in case your soul would revive and be renewed before you died, but it's too late." Her eyes—too bright to see— bore into Tammy, finding me somewhere inside her. *Is it now? Or is it yet to be?*

What? Tammy asked, but I was the one who jumped. She was talking to me. The guardian angel who had been with Tammy was talking to me. She knew I was here, living the future, and the angel didn't know if what we were living was true, or just a maybe. God, I hoped it was a maybe.

A shadow covered the window, and the stink of wet stone. My pulse leapt as I saw the black wing slide into the room through the open window. Fear hit me, sour and rank, and

Paul sensed my sudden terror.

"Her soul is dead, Madison," the guardian angel said to me, not a hint of accusation in her voice. "It died three years ago, and I stayed with her, keeping the black wings from her in the hope that it might rekindle and grow anew, but it did not. She failed to nourish it, and it perished utterly."

No! I shouted as the first black wing landed on her.

Tammy screamed, her body dead but something still aware in her. White-hot ice filled her thoughts, peppermint and fire. I tried to pull back, but I was caught in this hell and couldn't escape. Black wings had found her, and her memories were being eaten as we watched, unable to move and stop them. The energy that she had stored as memory was being stripped from her, the dripping sheet of black tearing memories from her like a hyena over a kill.

And like hyenas, more came. One by one, they fought their way into the room and covered Tammy as she screamed and writhed in her mind, unable to escape, unable to fight back, her body flaccid and still.

Stop! I pleaded, feeling real tears slip down my real cheeks somewhere across time in a dark graveyard. The memory of having my own thoughts stripped from me returned, and I felt anew the burning lack, the fear of nothing being left behind. She was being taken apart, aware and watching. *This?* I thought in horror. *This is what happens to lost souls? No wonder dark reapers kill them.*

Someone please help me! Tammy screamed, her body peaceful but her mind in terror as huge chunks of her disappeared. She was becoming nothing. I couldn't help her, and I cried, huge racking sobs as I tried to hold her together, failing.

Not this! I said, fighting off a black wing when the image of a sun-drenched car from Tammy's memories filled me. There was laughter, a silly song. Nothing much, but there was happiness. This they couldn't take, and I pulled it to me, hoarding it.

The black wing I took it from rose up, and I howled as it fought me for it, hungry and having gotten a taste. I shoved a memory to it, one just as precious but one of mine. The black wing melted into nothing, not knowing the difference. I curled myself around Tammy's beautiful memory, crying and wishing it would all just end.

Slowly Tammy's agony and terror ebbed as more and more was taken, and less and less was left, and finally it was just Paul and me. One by one, the black wings lifted, swollen and mis-shapen as they staggered out the open window, bumping into the glass like wasps until they found their way. My thoughts shaky, I reached for Paul's presence, feeling like a great tide of poison had rolled over us and only we had survived. The guardian angel was still with us, her tears now ceased as the one she watched and protected, in the slim hope her soul would renew itself, vanished as if she had never existed. Hope, that's all the light reapers bought with their guardian angels, a slim hope that the soul would rekindle. It was a hope that Barnabas had started with his beautiful Sarah, and heartache filled me at the travesty of it.

"Has this happened yet?" the angel asked me, her voice sad. "I can't tell. Has *this* happened yet? Is it happening now? You've never been here before at the end."

I felt raw, and even though I knew I was really sitting in a graveyard, I also knew I was here, in the future, talking to Tammy's guardian angel that she didn't have yet. *It hasn't happened,* I thought, feeling emotionally drained. Cupped in the curve of my awareness was one bright spot of glory—Tammy's memory too beautiful to allow to be eaten.

The angel rose up, her eyes going terrible and hard. "Make it stop," she said, and it was as if she carried the voice of God in her. "Please," she added, sounding helpless now. And then she vanished.

The world flashed red, and I let out a choking sob of relief. It was over, and I steadied myself for the gut-wrenching feeling of my consciousness being yanked back across the years of what-if to reality.

I woke up crying, curled up on the wet grass between Nakita and Barnabas, Josh standing awkwardly as if not knowing how he could help. They were silent and subdued, knowing that it had to be bad by the shape I was in. Meeting their eyes, I saw the tears in Nakita's. Barnabas had cried his last eons ago, but the pain behind his gaze was no less. He had started this when Sarah's soul had revived. I didn't know if I should thank or curse him. It was awful.

Sitting up, I looked for Paul. He was standing hunched beside a distant tombstone, puking his guts out. "I'm sorry," I whispered, and he turned, wiping his mouth. Haggard, he faced me, looking more alone than I'd ever seen a person. I tried to get up, and Josh jumped to help. My hand was cold in his, and shaking.

"Are you okay?" I asked Paul, hearing my voice crack. "That was a bad one."

"No." His word was short, full of the dead terror we had endured. "That . . ." he said, hands shaking as he tried to find words. "That was hell. This job is hell!"

I couldn't find fault with him there, and I staggered, listing sideways until Josh pulled me upright. "It's not always like that," I breathed. *Sometimes you're burned alive.*

Paul turned away, his expression ugly as he tried to come to grips with what we had seen. I leaned against a rock—excuse me . . . a grave marker—and Josh let go after making sure I wasn't going to fall over. "You okay?" he asked, and I nodded, not looking up at him.

"It was a flash forward," I said, and Barnabas sighed, seeming to know what I'd seen. "We saw Tammy's death. A few years from now, I'm guessing. I don't know. She had a guardian angel so I think if we walk away right now, we fail to help her." My words drifted to nothing as I thought back to what the angel had said to me.

"We have to do something," I said, remembering the pain Tammy ended her life with, and then the utter nothingness, a nothing so complete that it was as if she had never existed. "If we can't help her, Tammy's life is worthless, no grace, no beauty. She didn't do anything to nourish her soul. No art, no creativity, taking in nothing outside of eating, sleeping, living, and when she died, her soul was eaten by black wings."

Bile rose, and I forced it back. She was gone. Except for the tiny bit I had kept. I could feel it in me, lost, alone, and not fitting in with the rest of my memories.

Nakita touched my arm and I jumped. Her eyes were brimming with tears, but it only made her more beautiful. "I'm sorry, Madison. I thought you knew that's what happened to lost souls if they can't rekindle them. That's why I was so confused. Rekindled souls happen so rarely. So very rarely." She was looking at Barnabas. His head was down, and it looked as if he was reliving his entire lifetime of lonely heartache.

"I didn't know!" I shouted, and he looked up, tears in his eyes. "I didn't know," I said softly. "No one told me." I glanced at Paul. Clearly he hadn't known, either. My sorrow was shifting to anger, but it didn't feel any better.

"That's why we take them early," Nakita said, giving Barnabas a soft glance. "To spare them that and save what we can. If Tammy is scythed tonight, a light reaper will keep her soul safe until she is welcomed home, remembered, loved. Like Barnabas was going to do for you until you stole Kairos's amulet.

But if she is given a guardian angel and her soul doesn't rekindle itself . . ."

I finished Nakita's thought for her. "A life of nothing, ending in the same."

I turned from them, heartsick and confused. Maybe I should just give up and send reapers to cull souls.

"I can't do this."

It had come from Paul, and I looked up at him, his features hidden in shadow.

"I can't be the light timekeeper," he said. "This is insane!" He started to back away into the dark. "I can't do it! I can't!"

Barnabas pressed his lips together. Reaching out, he grabbed Paul's arm. "You are the rising light timekeeper."

"I don't want it!" Paul said, panicking but unable to break Barnabas's hold. "I can't *do* that! I can't send reapers out to put guardian angels on people if all they are going to do is be eaten by that sludge! It would be better if they died young!"

My head dropped as Paul struggled to unwedge himself from Barnabas's grip, finally managing it and stepping back as he rubbed his arm. And that was where we were. Neither of us wanted to do what was expected of us. I knew I should be depressed, but a part of me was glad I wasn't the only one being asked to do something I didn't want to do. Together, maybe, we could do what one of us could not.

"Listen to me!" Barnabas said, his hand on his amulet as if it was the hilt of his sword. "You are the rising light timekeeper!

You will keep your mouth shut. You will learn what Ron teaches you. You will take his amulet when he steps down!"

"Barnabas!" Nakita exclaimed, appalled.

Barnabas ignored her. "And when you reach your power, you will use your understanding of choice to change things," he finished.

Josh exhaled in understanding, and I stiffened. Barnabas turned his gaze to me, and I shivered at the depth of his heartache. Eons of it, stored behind his dark eyes. "You both will," he said to me, his voice breaking. "We just have to be patient."

"I don't want to wait a lifetime to make a difference," I said.

"Then you find them when you can," Barnabas said, a new, almost eerie fervor to his voice that bordered on the fanatical. "Talk to them if they listen. *Before* Ron sends an angel to guard them or the seraphs send a reaper to scythe them."

It was what I had been trying to do all along. Barnabas believed it was possible. Maybe now, Paul did, too. And if Paul did, perhaps we had a real chance.

"We have to find Tammy," Paul said, his voice almost virulent. "We have to change this. She can't be allowed to live her life if all that is at the end of it is . . . for the sum of her life and memories to be eaten by a mindless dish of bacteria!"

"Then we do this?" I said, hope making me shake inside.

Paul took a breath, knowing he was agreeing to more than saving Tammy. He was going to get in trouble. Ron wasn't going to be happy. Screw Ron.

"We do this," Paul said. His eyes closed briefly, and then he turned to look deeper into the graveyard, across it to the rest of the town. "She's not very far away."

"Good," Nakita said, her expression drawn up into a worried look. "Because Demus is gone."

ELEVEN

It wasn't the muggy, breathless darkness that creeped me out and made my stomach clench. It wasn't that I couldn't hear Barnabas and Nakita behind me somewhere, swords drawn as they jogged after me. It wasn't that my out-of-shape breathing was harsh and heavy next to Josh's long-distance runner's light breaths. It wasn't even that this end of town had bars on the windows and roll-down gates over the storefronts. What bothered me was that I was still barefoot and had stepped in something sticky.

Grimacing, I raised my foot and shuddered.

"This way," Barnabas said, easing past me as I hesitated. I could hardly see him in the black alley, his coat making him a moving shadow. Nakita's scent brushed past me, and I started to follow. Paul edged past Josh and me, and I couldn't help but see how predatory the two reapers looked beside him: Barnabas dark and furtive, Nakita taut and slim, both on the hunt, both joined in thought to one goal. I was proud of them, working together like that. Demus's amulet was in my pocket, heavy and warm. I don't know what he intended to do to Tammy without it, but Demus and Tammy were together according to Barnabas.

"She's just ahead," Paul whispered as he turned, the streetlight glinting on the shine of his dress shoes. His posture was tense and eager, and I wished I could see the time line to gauge how close we were.

The brighter square of black at the end of the alley beckoned; I picked up my pace. "Watch it!" Josh whispered, reaching out and jerking me back an instant before I stepped in a foul-smelling pile of garbage outside a side door.

It was a bad part of town. I wouldn't come here even during the day. The street was empty, seeing as it was about two in the morning. A faint brightening hinted at the coming sunrise, but it was hours off. The air stank, heavy and humid. Streetlights barely lit the potholed street, the asphalt making hardly any division between itself and the sidewalk, and then the tired, chipped buildings with their roll-down gates and bricked-up windows. It was rock, asphalt, and cement. Not a hint of anything green or alive. Not even a rat.

Which is probably a good thing, I thought as I shifted my weight from one cold foot to the other. "Thanks," I whispered back, wrinkling my nose at the smell. My arms had gone around my middle, and I was cold. Maybe I should have waited until we were done with this prevention before claiming my body. And what was that squishy thing between my toes? This was just gross.

"She's in there," Paul said, his rising chin indicating a bus depot, the broken neon sign in the shape of a big arrow.

"With Demus," Nakita said, almost hissing the word.

"The bus depot," I said, turning to give Josh a smile. "You were right."

Heart pounding, I took a step forward only to have Barnabas yank me back. Overhead, a streetlight popped to put us in darkness. My eyes went up as I wondered if it was Grace, and Barnabas whispered, "Cop car."

Frustrated, I pulled back into the even darker alley. Paul was beside me and Josh. Nakita jumped straight up, vanishing onto the roof. The slow sound of an idling engine grew, and we pressed back even more, hiding behind a box. I could see inside the bus depot from where I stood with my back to the wall. Demus and Tammy were just talking, but I was sure if Demus had had his amulet, she'd be dead by now.

It *was* a cop car, and I silently thanked Grace for the broken light as it cruised very slowly past, the spotlight playing over the abandoned storefronts and probing into the dark places.

Standing between me and the top of the alley, Paul exhaled as the car slowly drove away. He looked determined as he shifted to the center of the alley, and I couldn't help but feel a spark of something as we all followed him back to the street. *Not romantic but perhaps a contemporary?* I wondered. Someone who would really understand the hell that we had to go through. That is, if I kept my amulet.

"He's gone," Paul said as the cop's brake lights flashed and the car turned a corner.

"Do you think they're looking for me?" I asked, reluctant to step into the open.

Barnabas was a shadow on my other side, his gaze still where the car had disappeared. "Probably no. I tweaked their memories of you. I *think* I got everyone."

Paul turned to frown at him. "You *think*?"

Barnabas frowned right back. "Nothing is certain."

"The car is gone," I said, tension making me jittery. "Let's go."

"Black wings!" Paul said, and I froze, fighting an irrational fear as I looked up, seeing their black outlines against the sooty sky. There was a flash of brilliant light as one turned, and I looked away, shivering. I had a body. They couldn't sense me. And even if they could, they couldn't touch me. Not with a real aura around me again.

"What are they doing here?" Josh asked, hunched and uneasy. He'd seen what they had done to me. "Demus can't scythe anyone if you have his amulet. And they don't follow light reapers." He looked at Barnabas, his expression ill. "Right?"

Barnabas said nothing as he put a hand on my shoulder and pushed us into motion. "Not usually, no. But we've got three reapers, a timekeeper, and a rising timekeeper out here. Even plants turn to the sun."

And maybe Arariel was here hunting, too, I mused, following us since she couldn't find Tammy on her own. My eyes scanning everything, we crossed the empty street, moving furtively and avoiding going right under the circling black sheets of dripping goo. God, I hated those things, and I shivered at the memory of them eating Tammy's memories until she was nothing.

"What is Demus even doing here?" I babbled, mincing in my bare feet. "He can't make a scythe."

"I think he's going to push her in front of a bus."

I looked askance at Barnabas, trying to decide if he was being funny or not.

There was the soft sound of feathers, and a soft click of heels, and Nakita joined us as we reached the door. I pulled one side of the twin doors only to find it locked. Barnabas reached in front of me and gave a yank. With a sharp ping of breaking metal, the door opened. A fetid scent of old sneakers and stale cigarettes spilled out. Nice.

Demus looked up. His boyish features—softened to lull Tammy—became hard. "Broken feathers and pinions, get behind me, Tam!" he said as he stood, pushing her behind himself.

Frightened, the girl stood, holding his shoulders and peeping around his shoulder. "Oh, there's a good idea," Barnabas said as he filed in behind me.

"Tammy, honey, his job is to kill you," Nakita said, taking my other side.

It was clear Tammy had been crying; her eyes were red and her hair was a mess. There was a backpack beside her. It was likely all she had in the world—apart from her soul. She was running. It was the beginning of the end for her, and I had to stop it here. If she left, she'd believe the lies she was telling herself, and her soul would die.

"He is not going to hurt me!" she exclaimed as she took in the five of us, but she was edging back as if unsure. "You burned my apartment. He's going to—"

"Save you?" I said, and she looked up at him, seeing his anger at us and her doubt grew. "Take you away from everything? Tammy, he's lying. Angels do that." I glanced at Barnabas, adding, "A lot."

A frown crossed Barnabas's face, and he pulled to a stop from where he had been edging away from us, trying to circle Demus. Nakita had been doing the same on the right. "Especially dark reapers," Barnabas said, looking at his nails, feigning disinterest. I could tell he was poised to move in an eyeblink.

"Then why hasn't Demus killed me already?" she asked belligerently.

"Because I have his sword," I said, pulling his amulet out and dangling it.

"Madison, no!" Barnabas yelled, but Demus had seen it, and lunged, exactly as I had wanted.

Nakita made a dart for Tammy, pushing her back to a bulletin board and getting between her and Demus. Josh reached out and pulled me out of the way, and Paul danced clear, his shiny shoes clacking.

"Oh, crap!" Josh yelled as his tug caused my fingers, cold and damp, to slip on the lanyard. The flat black stone glittered as it arced through the air, and a delicate ting of crystal echoed for one pure instant when it hit the floor.

"Barnabas! Get it!" I yelled as I fell, but Demus had already switched directions and was diving for it. I watched breathlessly as Paul got there first.

"I got it!" he shouted triumphantly, then his eyes widened at the sight of Demus barreling toward him. Knowing he didn't have a chance, he threw it to Nakita.

"Here!" the dark reaper shouted, hand raised, but it wasn't her grip that the stone landed in. It was Arariel's.

"Son of a puppy!" I shouted as I scrambled up, and she smiled pure evil at me, pulling back out of Nakita's sword's reach.

"I'm sorry!" Josh was saying, his hands on my shoulders as we blocked the door.

"I'm the one who dropped it," I said, frustrated as I tugged my oversize shirt straight.

"Arariel! Give me the amulet!" Paul demanded, but she wasn't listening to him, twirling Demus's amulet like she'd won a prize at the fair.

"Nakita?" I questioned, and my wonderful reaper grinned just as evilly back, her sword dipping once in invitation to Arariel. Behind Nakita, Tammy curled into a ball in one of the flaccid-cushioned chairs against the wall, crying. I really couldn't blame her.

"You will not grace her with a guardian angel," Nakita intoned, and Arariel fell into a fighting stance, poised.

"And I'm not going to let you kill her, foul black reaper!" she shouted back, lunging.

"You call me foul?" Nakita shouted, face red. "I give a clean release, not a slow death! You are ugly. Ugly!"

Demus just wanted his amulet, still dangling from Arariel's hand. He watched it hungrily, inching closer as Nakita pushed Arariel farther from Tammy. I jumped when Barnabas touched my shoulder. "You and Josh get Tammy out of here," he whispered. "She's too scared to move. I'll stay here and try to help Nakita."

Scared was right. I could be killed now, and I knew the feeling. Josh looked as unsettled as I was, but he gave my hand a quick squeeze, and together we circled around Nakita and Arariel as they took their first shots at each other.

Tammy's tear-streaked face turned to us as we approached, and she scrunched back into the chair when I reached for her.

"Come on!" I exclaimed. "We have to get out of here!"

Tammy kicked at me, and I jumped back. "Shoe said you were dead," she said, terrified. "Are you dead?"

"Come on, Madison . . ." Josh urged, standing between me and the reapers.

She called him! I thought, elated. "I used to be," I said quickly. "But I'm not anymore, which is why we have to get out of here!" How could she believe I was dead, and still trust Demus's lies? Again I grabbed her wrist, and this time she let me pull her to her feet.

"Look out!" Paul shouted, and we ducked as a chair ripped from the floor crashed into the wall only five feet away, bits of tile and cement peppering us like shrapnel. Nakita was getting serious.

"We gotta go," Josh said, and we ran for the door.

Arariel saw us. Battle cry ringing, she leapt high, circling over Nakita's sword to land between us and the door. My eyes widened, and I pushed Tammy behind me as we skidded to a halt.

"Arariel, stop!" Paul called out from the opposite side of the room.

"You are not my keeper," she snarled, then looked to the ceiling. "Heaven's guard, descend!" she called out, summoning a guardian angel.

Oh, crap. If an angel was assigned, then it was all over! "Back!" I shouted, but Tammy had frozen where she stood, frightened.

Demus lunged at Arariel, intent on his amulet. Bellowing, he crashed into her, and they went down as she screamed in outrage. Demus's black stone hit the tile floor, flashing violet for an instant as it bounced. Flat on his stomach, Demus reached, stretched, and got it. With a cry of relief, he rolled to a stand, his blade already forming.

Teeth clenched, Nakita swung at Demus, her lips pulled back and the glory of heaven in her eyes. Their blades met, and again a clear ping of infinity rang.

My heart was pounding, and Paul slid to a stop beside us, his eyes bright. "Arariel isn't listening to me," he said, sounding betrayed.

"You think?" Josh said, finally getting Tammy to move back a step as she watched the angels battle for her soul.

"We have got to get out of here!" I said. "Tammy, we have to go!"

Barnabas was at the door, holding it open and making frantic "out" gestures, but Nakita, Demus, and Arariel were too close for my comfort.

"My God," Tammy whispered, the tears stopped in her awe. "Shoe wasn't lying."

"Her!" Arariel cried out, kicking both Demus and Nakita back so she could point her sword at Tammy. "She is heaven's blessed. Save her!"

Oh, shit, it was the angel. Without thought, I reached out with one hand and shoved Tammy behind me. With the other,

I grabbed Paul's hand. My head snapped back as the battle suddenly took on a new hue of sparkle and depth as I saw everything with the added power of his amulet. Deep tones shook the air at each blow, and energy radiated from the battling reapers like the sun. And over it all were two small glowing balls of light. One was Grace, and the other was the one from my flash forward.

"No!" I cried out, hand raised to the guardian angel. "When I flashed forward, you told me to stop this, now I'm telling you! Leave! She is not to be graced with an angel!"

"She is the one!" Arariel shouted, then dropped her sword and gripped her wrist with a cry as Nakita finally scored on her.

"She is mine!" I said, words flowing from me in desperation. Tammy's future death rang through me, the terrible futility of a life wasted making me frantic.

"Please!" Tammy cried out, hiding behind Josh, clutching at him as he stood in front of her. "Go away! All of you! I just want to live. I want to live!"

"That's a start," Paul said.

"Come with me, and you will," Arariel said, her hand outstretched. Behind her, Nakita and Demus got to their feet, blades out but pointing down. They didn't attack, feeling the power of the guardian angel soak into them. It was up to me now. Could I convince the angel that Tammy was mine, or would that awful future of a life wasted be true?

The angel waited, recognizing me, but probably not knowing

if this was the moment of now, the future, or even the past. Outside, the black wings gathered. One plastered itself against the window, and I shuddered. Paul tried to pull away, but I gripped his hand harder. If he let go, I'd lose sight of the guardian angel.

"That is not life you offer her," I said to Arariel, pulling my gaze from the ugly sight. "It's a slow death. You can't have her. She is already mine!" I took a breath, feeling wild and unreal. "I am the dark timekeeper, and I have claimed her, I say she is not to be scythed, and she is *not* to be graced with a guardian. She is mine!"

"Claimed her?" Arariel said, her stance losing its confidence. "You can't claim her!"

"I have," I said, shaking as I remembered Tammy's death and how I had exchanged part of my soul for hers to keep it from being eaten. "I have a part of her soul," I said, and Tammy whimpered, pressing into Josh. "She's dark now. She is part of the dark, and the light has no claim." I leaned toward Arariel, my voice low as I said, "You can't touch her."

Tammy's eyes widened, and even Josh looked shocked. I was too afraid to look at Paul, standing beside me as I gripped his arm.

"You?" Arariel was thunderstruck. "You claim her soul?"

"Leave!" I shouted, gesturing, and Arariel leapt backward, yelping and holding a hand to her chest as if burned.

"I thought your amulet didn't work," Paul said.

"It doesn't," I said, confused. "I didn't do anything."

"It was the old power," Arariel said, hunched as she backed away, giving the guardian angel a betrayed glare. "Ancient law, you speak of the ancient law, your claim surmounting heaven's itself. I can't touch her! *I can't touch her!*"

Nakita, too, looked shocked, scared almost, as she dissolved her sword. "Madison?" Nakita warbled. "What have you done?"

"Look out!" Barnabas shouted, and I tripped on the cuffs of my too-long pants and fell back as Arariel wailed, stretching her shoulders until her wings flashed into existence and took up the entire room. For an instant they brushed the edges of the walls, and then, still keening, she wrapped them around herself and vanished in a thunderous clap of sound.

Stunned, I looked over the destruction, racks of chairs upended, holes in the ceiling, and deep gouges in the floor from divine swords. Nakita rose from a crouch, halfway across the room. "Where did you learn the ancient law?" she whispered. "Madison, you are responsible for her soul now. If it fails to thrive, you will be held accountable. Do you know what that means?"

Not really, but I could make some guesses. I was scared, becoming more so as Barnabas growled at her to shut up. The guardian angel was gone. Or at least I didn't see her. I'd lost my grip on Paul when I'd fallen, and he had backed away, his arm behind his back as if I was going to take it again. Maybe that bit about me having a piece of Tammy's soul had scared him.

It didn't make me feel very warm and fuzzy, either—even if it had saved her life. Frightened, I tried to reach his eyes, but he was making a huge effort to avoid me, head down as he tucked his shirt back in.

From the floor, Tammy stared at the empty space where Arariel had been. Her mouth was hanging open. She wasn't crying. She wasn't scared. She looked numb. "She . . ." Tammy started, then swallowed hard. "She had wings. Are you all angels?"

"Just them," Josh said, pointing to Barnabas and Nakita. Demus was gone. Swell. But the black wings were, too, and I breathed a sigh of relief. "Did you save her?" Josh asked me, and I nodded, taking his hand as he helped me up.

"Yes and no," I said as I glanced at Paul, who looked like he was avoiding me and wondering how much of this was going to end up in Ron's ears. It didn't feel over.

My bare feet seemed to find every pointy bit of broken tile and cement, and I shifted uneasily as Nakita set an overturned chair upright and sat in it, her elbows on her knees as she caught her breath. Grime marred her white clothes, making her gray, turning her black. This mess was going to be hard to explain. But then again, in this part of town, maybe not.

"Are you okay?" Nakita asked from across the room, and I nodded, feeling Josh's touch on me slip away. We were okay—for now. Arariel wasn't going to forget this had happened, and Demus was going to go crying to the seraphs. . . .

Barnabas reached out to help Tammy to her feet. She stared

at his hand for a moment, then, when he smiled, she slipped her hand into his and stood. A pang hit me, and I watched as she dropped her eyes, suddenly shy as she realized he was an angel. I'd been the same way, and I wondered at my past innocence.

"Is it true?" Paul accused harshly, jerking me from my thoughts. "Is it true what you said about having part of her soul? Is that why they can't touch her? Because you tied her soul to your own?"

My lips parted, and I glanced at Tammy, still with Barnabas. "I'm trying to help," I whispered, tugging my oversize shirt straight again. It wouldn't stay put.

"You said you claimed my soul? That you had it?" Tammy said, the beginnings of trust that Barnabas had started dropping from her.

"Just a tiny piece of it," I said, almost pleading. "Tammy, I saw you in the future, dying. The black wings were eating you alive! I couldn't let them take everything. You had such beautiful memories of your mother and Johnny; I couldn't bear to see them destroyed forever even though you'd forgotten them. I gave the black wings one of my memories instead. *They took a part of me instead!* They ate it, and it's gone forever. If I could give you yours back, I would, but I don't know how!"

"They eat me alive . . ." Tammy breathed, fixated on that one part and backing away. Making a tiny cry, she turned and ran for the door.

"Tammy! We're trying to help!" I called out, but Barnabas was faster, and he was in front of her before she got halfway there.

"Wait," he said, grabbing her.

"Help!" she screamed, hitting him. "Someone help me!"

I felt awful, and I winced when Tammy smacked his face, leaving a handprint on his cheek. "It's okay," he whispered, pulling her closer, comforting her. "They won't eat you now. You're not the same. It's going to be okay. You belong to the dark now."

"But I don't want to belong to the dark!" she wailed, slumping into his warmth and his strength, feeling the purity of him and taking comfort in it. Her cries for help dissolved into racking sobs, and he held her firm.

I knew how she felt.

Paul looked at me, his disgust at my having stolen a piece of her future soul starting to evaporate. Josh touched my elbow, and I jumped. "If you gave them part of your own, then isn't that okay?" Josh asked, his eyebrows high. "You saved a little bit of her, didn't you?"

"I think she might have saved all of her," Nakita said as she stood up.

It was starting to look like I might have, but at what cost? Ancient law. It sounded like I was responsible for her now, I guess. If her soul died, would I be the one to suffer, not her? Guess I'd better make sure her soul didn't die.

Tammy's sobs quieted, and I wondered if there were any more

tissues in Nakita's purse. I took a breath to ask her when she sidled up to me, but everything went out of my head when Nakita leaned close and whispered, "Grace has a message for you."

It was as if my heart seemed to stop. My head snapped up, and I looked over the destruction. "W-what?" I asked, my knees going weak.

"Uh, she says they want to talk to you."

They? "They who?" I asked, already guessing she meant the seraphs. I'd taken part of Tammy's soul. That probably wasn't a good thing in hindsight, even if it had saved her. I think it had saved her. I looked at Tammy, shaken and distraught as Josh and Barnabas talked to her. *Please, let it have saved her?*

Nakita looked at one of the ceiling lights, and it glowed brighter. Grace. "The seraphs," she said, looking frightened. "You're to go to Ron's."

Josh looked up from Tammy. "You mean the light time-keeper?" he exclaimed. "No way!"

My gaze went to Paul, seeing that he was just as scared as I was. Clearly they knew I'd gotten Paul to help me. And now that I'd gotten my body back, they were likely going to insist that I give back the amulet after the mess I'd made here.

Barnabas gently pushed Tammy from his shoulder, handing her a black handkerchief. "That was quick."

"I thought we might have a little time," Paul said nervously, and I realized just how many lives I'd messed up trying to save one.

"I'm so sorry," I said, looking at them in turn. "Paul, I didn't mean to get you in this much trouble."

"No," he said firmly, his gaze going haunted as he glanced away. "I'd do it again in a second. The system in place is flawed. I stand by what I believe." He shifted his feet, frightened but determined. "It's okay. I'll be with you."

"No you won't." Nakita grimaced as the light that surrounded Grace fizzed and hummed. "You're staying here with Tammy to take her home."

"I'm not leaving her now!" I said loudly. "This is just so they can come back and kill her or slap a guardian angel on her! Which in this case is the same thing!" My thoughts winged back to the guardian angel crying over Tammy, and the thunder in her voice when she told me to change things. That had to mean something. It *had* to!

Tammy's expression flashed into fear again. "Don't leave me. Please!" she said, clutching at Barnabas. "I don't know what's going on! I just want to go home!"

"Home is exactly where Paul is going to take you," Nakita said, just as loudly. Glaring at the light she added, "I'm telling her! Shut up!" With a huff, she turned to me. "Paul is to take Tammy home. Uh, I mean to her aunt's, where her mother is staying." She looked at Tammy with hard severity. "They are worried sick about you."

"I'm sorry." Tammy's voice was a faint whisper of real regret, and in it I felt a breath of hope. Maybe she had changed. Maybe she was going to live, touch the lives around her for the better and not just exist.

"Barnabas is going to take Josh home," Nakita said, and Josh stiffened in protest. "And I," Nakita said, "am going to take you to Ron's. It's almost sunrise there, and the seraphs like the sunrise." She focused on me, and her eyes pinched in concern. "They know you have your body back."

Damn it, I was in so much trouble. But I wouldn't change a thing. The light surrounding Grace popped and went out, startling me. Swallowing hard, I turned to Paul. "You'll get her home?"

Paul walked across to Tammy, his hand extended. "I'm not as pretty as Barnabas, but I can tell you what's going on. I've seen your future."

She blinked, the tears almost starting again. "Is it okay?" she warbled.

Turning to the door, Paul started to lead her away, stepping over and around chunks of ceiling tile and foam from the seats. "That depends upon what you do. The future isn't fixed, you know. You have the choice of your fate. I can tell you what I saw. And then I'll tell you what could happen if you change a little. Open up and see things differently."

The knot in my chest started to ease. If I was going to lose my timekeeper status, I'd at least leave with the satisfaction of having saved Tammy's life. That is, if they let me remember it.

The door to the bus depot squeaked as it opened, and then

it fell in a sliding crash to hang from one hinge. Tammy and Paul gingerly stepped around it. Paul turned, holding Tammy's hand. "If I don't see you again, Barnabas, I'm sorry for calling you grim. You're still light. I don't care what color your amulet is."

Barnabas ducked his head, seeming to grow taller. "I'm not," he said, eyes holding determination when they rose, flicking first to me, then Paul. "But thank you."

Paul nodded and turned back to Tammy. Together they walked down the street, his voice rising and falling as he told her what he had seen in her future.

Slowly my smile faded as my reality soaked in. I had royally messed up. Taken a slice of someone else's soul. That had to be illegal or something. They were going to take my amulet. Make me forget. Ancient law, Arariel had said. That didn't sound good. Cold, I wrapped my arms around myself and looked at the busted light. "Is Grace coming?" I asked, knowing I'd feel better if she was.

"She's here." Barnabas moved closer to stand beside me. He shook his shoulders, and his long coat shimmered, growing into his black-feathered wings. "I'm taking you to Ron's," he said. "Nakita can take Josh home."

"The seraphs—" Nakita said, and Barnabas glared, leaning until they were nose to nose.

"I. Am. Taking. Her." Barnabas leaned back, losing his threatening mien. "See you around, Josh."

But would he? I didn't know.

"Madison?" Josh said, his voice uneasy.

Shaky and light-headed, I gave him a hug. "Thanks for being here," I whispered, pressing into him as if he was the only thing real anymore. "I don't know what's going to happen. I hope I don't forget."

"Me either," he said as he stepped back and we parted.

Then I glanced up as Grace's light doubled in brightness.

"I'm . . . sorry."

"For what?" I said, and Barnabas cleared his throat for us to hurry up.

Josh smiled sickly at me. "I wanted this to work. I know it meant a lot to you."

My stomach hurt, and I couldn't look at him. "See you at home," I said, and Barnabas tugged me to him.

Biting my lip so I wouldn't cry, I leaned back into Barnabas as his wings enfolded me, and with a sudden feeling of falling, the bus depot melted away and we were gone.

TWELVE

My feet slipped off Barnabas's, and I gasped, clutching at his arm wrapped around me as my toes dangled in the wind. The world shifted beneath us, wheeling as an updraft buoyed us higher. I was safer in Barnabas's grip than I would be at home in my own room. More so, probably.

"I've got you," he murmured in my ear, a mix of annoyance and reassurance that only Barnabas could manage. Flying was a lot scarier now that hitting the ground held real consequence. I still had the bruises from hitting the seat belt. I didn't need to add to them.

"I trust you," I said, squinting down at the desert below. "It's me I'm worried about."

He said nothing, but his flight smoothed into a slow spiral down. It looked like he was headed for the modest home below us. Ron's, presumably. It was the same color as the tan, almost pink sand. There was nearly no vegetation, either next to the house or in the surrounding area. I didn't see any roads at all leading up to it, and no sign of people anywhere. Just a low single-story adobe home amid the desert dirt and water-cut gullies.

It was quiet and dim; the sun wasn't up yet, but it was close. The wind was a steady, dry force, blowing my hair first one way, then another as Barnabas circled to a pink-tiled patio that opened seamlessly to the desert. My nerves were ragged. I didn't know what was going to happen in the next five minutes, but it was tearing me up that I might not have a chance to even say good-bye. They'd let me say good-bye, wouldn't they?

I was pretty sure I was meeting with the seraphs for one of three reasons: one, I stole some of Tammy's soul; two, because I convinced the rising light timekeeper to help me circumvent a guardian angel; or three, to give them my amulet back and renounce my timekeeper status because I got my body back. But the seraph had said I could do that if I *chose* to. What if I *chose* to do something different now?

Maybe we hadn't succeeded with Tammy. Maybe we had. Wasn't it worth spending a little time to find out? And if it became certain that she would never change, then I would scythe her down myself.

Oh, God. Could I do that?

Barnabas set us down with a gentle step-hop, and I let out

my held breath. His grip on me loosened, and I turned. I knew I had a scared look on my face, but he managed to muster up a weak smile for me. "I'll see you later," Barnabas said, and I reached for his sleeve, keeping him from going more than a step.

"You're not staying?" My voice quavered, and I hated it.

Sighing, he dropped his head, then looked back up at me. "I can't. I have to leave. I hope . . . I hope I see you later."

They were going to take my amulet from me. I knew it. And my hand grabbed it, useless as it was at this point. "Remember me," I breathed.

Barnabas cupped my chin, his thumb wiping away a tear that had somehow leaked out. "If they let me," he said. "You were a very good timekeeper, Madison."

Barnabas's hand dropped. Eyes fixed to mine, he backed up. His wings made one fast downward push, and he was airborne. I felt alone and miserable.

He'd been told to leave, and he left. Angels were made to serve, Barnabas had said. But if one served unwillingly, wasn't it slavery?

A bitter resolve pushed out my fear as I watched his silhouette spin, turn, and vanish. Sure, I had made the deal to give the amulet back once I had my body, but things had changed. I—no, *we*—had proved that a soul's fate was not fixed, but that it could be turned back to a better path. I wanted my body, my amulet, and a chance to really see if this could work, and as I turned to look at Ron's house, I promised myself that I wasn't going to let anything go without a fight.

Arms wrapped around myself, I looked in the wide patio doors at a huge, tiled living room done in tasteful browns, taupes, and pale pinks and oranges. It looked very desert-ish, so unlike my green suburbia. No wonder Ron wore desert robes; the sand must get into everything.

Going up and knocking didn't seem right—after all, the sun wasn't up yet—and it wasn't like I wanted to talk to Ron. "Where are you?" I whispered, looking up into the pale blue sky that almost looked white. No seraphs.

I went to sit on the waist-high wall surrounding most of the patio, angling so that I could see the house and the rising sun both. I'd never been to the desert, and it was breathtaking in its open beauty. The horizon was so far away, the colors melting into themselves like watercolors. The wind blew into me as if it had never brushed against anything ever before. I could feel a hum in my veins, and I wondered if it was because the ground was holy. It would have to be for a seraph to set foot on it. My island, too, was holy.

A thump on the glass door shattered my introspective mood, and I spun, chest clenching when I saw Ron, furious as he struggled to get the door to slide open. "You!" he shouted, his bony, bare, ugly feet slapping as he came out. "Paul is gone. You're here. What have you done with him?" His pace slowed as he noticed my new, reaper-black clothes.

I slid from the wall and tugged my oversize tunic straight. "Hi, Ron. Nice place you have. Must be a bitch getting out here with no roads. Or is that to keep people from leaving once they get here?"

I gasped, backpedaling as he reached for me, giving me a shake with his small hands on my shoulders. I was too taken aback to try to stop him, and besides, I thought I deserved it.

"The seraphs told me to come here," I said, teeth rattling. "Not my idea. I'm waiting for them! Get your . . . hands off!"

Ron let go, backing up as he tried to guess if I was telling the truth. His eyes narrowed in the rising sun, he looked at me. "You're alive," he said suddenly, and his gaze dropped to my amulet.

"Yeah," I said in a huff. "I found my body. Thanks for adding to the misery."

"I'm not going to adjust your amulet if that's why you're here," Ron said haughtily, backing up even more and slowly making a 360 with his gaze on the skies. "Where is Paul?"

Sniffing, I refused to let him know how miserable I was. Adjust my amulet? Adjust it right out of my hands, maybe. "Careful," I mocked, turning to look at the rising sun. "Someone might think you care about him."

"You little . . . girl," Ron spat, and I turned back around, hearing the hatred in his voice. "Where is Paul?! He's changed his amulet's signature. I don't know how, but he did. I can't find him."

My eyebrows rose. I hadn't told him how to change resonances, so his amulet must have changed on its own—because he helped me, the dark, save someone from the light. I didn't even try to hide my smug look, and Ron's look became choleric.

"You didn't!" Ron exclaimed. "How *dare* you interfere with my own student!"

"Why not? You interfered with me, and I was Kairos's student," I said, arms over my chest. "Well, I would have been his student if he hadn't been trying to *kill* me! Paul is helping me. We're saving souls."

"You are wrong, Madison." Standing stiffly before me, Ron fisted his hands, his eyes going blue for an instant as he touched the divine. "You cannot change a person's fate after their soul dies."

"You can if you catch them soon enough, before it dies completely!" I shouted, hearing my voice become lost in the desert, shredded by the wind. "What is your problem? You're the one who believes in choice. Or is it that you believe in choice only when it's done your way?"

Ron paced to me, and I stood firm, head even and lips pressed defiantly. "What did you do?!" he demanded.

"Nothing." I backed up a step, not liking him that close. My amulet wasn't working at all, and if I died before the seraph got here . . . well, who knew if it would listen to me, anyway. "Paul helped me find Tammy since my connection with my amulet is less than it should be. We flashed forward," I said, and

Ron's face went gray. "It wasn't happy-happy, Ron. We both saw what happens to the people you save with guardian angels who don't manage to rekindle their souls. Paul wasn't too thrilled about it. I wasn't, either. No wonder the dark timekeepers kill people to prevent that. I'm starting to think they are right. No one deserves to be eaten by black wings. Their entire existence erased like they never existed. When were you planning on telling him? When you were on your deathbed and you'd brainwashed him into being a second you?"

"You turned him dark . . ." It was a breathy whisper, but I could see the tension in him building.

"I did not!" I stated firmly, but I wondered. "We saw the truth! And the truth sucks!"

"You turned him dark!" he shouted, face going red. "He's my acolyte! You are toxic, Madison, poisoning everything you touch!"

"We were trying to save someone!" I shouted back, still holding myself like I was afraid. "Guardian angels are not guarding the living. They are guarding the dead in the vain hope that they will somehow rekindle their souls. People can't change unless they see the good and the bad. The light and the dark. The system doesn't work anymore!"

But he wasn't listening, his bony feet slapping the gritty pavers as he paced, his fury needing an outlet. "He was my student and you turned him against me!"

I took a breath to yell at him some more, but it came out in a gasp as he snatched his amulet, and a brilliant sword glittered into existence.

"Hey!" I shrieked, stepping backward to get space between us, but I stepped off the patio and into the soft sand. My arms pinwheeled and I went down. My air huffed out, and I could do nothing as he bore down on me, sword gleaming in the new sun.

I widened my eyes, and my breath sucked in as the sword glittered. And then Ron swung, his sword catching the first rays of the new day.

I'm going to die. Again, I thought, not knowing what that meant anymore. But a matte-black sword swung to block Ron's. The two met in a ping that was more feeling than sound, and I felt dizzy at the bubble of energy that was released, pressing out and away to color the sun and stir an echo from the sky itself. The sword above me looked as immutable as time, soaking in the light. My eyes struggled to shift, and I blinked at the seraph above me. I couldn't tell if it was the same one as before or not, the white glow hurting my eyes. Its face was terrible with anger, short of understanding and patience.

"Give me that," the seraph demanded, snatching Ron's sword from his slack grip.

Ron's sword in the seraph's hand made a ping, cracking from the hilt to the point. Ron stumbled back, his amulet on his chest glowing briefly before it went out. My lips parted at the new crack in the stone, leaking a silver line of infinity. Seeing it, Ron covered it, shamed.

But he was still angry.

I sat up at the seraph's feet, stunned. That awful black sword was gone, and the seraph was extending a hand to help me rise. Watching my hand move as if in a dream, I put my fingers out. It was a perfect hand, too strong to be feminine, but too thin to be masculine. And as I put mine into it, I could feel a divine strength humming, tightly leashed.

"Chronos? Is there an issue you wish to discuss?" the high angel said as it drew me effortlessly to my feet.

"She . . ." he stammered, eyes rising from his sword still in the seraph's hand. "She poisoned the rising light timekeeper against me!"

"Mmmm."

It was a slow sound, and I swear, I heard thunder rumble against the distant mountains, the seraph's thoughts echoing between heaven and earth. My pulse was fast, and I backed away from both of them, finding the patio and not knowing what to do with my hands. It had saved me, but saved me for what? They were going to take my amulet away.

"I'm sorry," I whispered, and both Ron and I took several prudent steps back as the angel moved to stand on the pavers as well. It was getting easier to look at it, and I snuck glances, its beauty still hurting me somehow.

"You showed Paul the truth of the guardian angels," the seraph said, looking too kindly at me for me to bear. "They are rejoicing that their torment finally be understood, and your praises are being sung whether anything changes or not. Paul made the choice he was fated to. Rest easy."

"That's not it," I said, and Ron made a frustrated noise.

"She turned him against me!" he protested. "My own student!"

I jumped when the angel abruptly looked at Ron. I hadn't even seen him move. Ron, too, had closed his mouth, scared. "You turned him against you yourself with your hoarding of knowledge in fear," the seraph said. "Be still for a moment. I want to know why Madison sorrows, and while here on earth, I can only do one thing at a time. It's bothersome. How do you exist able to do only one thing at a time, see one outcome from a thing instead of many?"

The seraph turned to me, concern pinching its brow to make it look more beautiful yet. "Madison, why do you sorrow?"

I couldn't look up, and I felt like I was before God himself. "I took some of Tammy's soul," I admitted. "In the flash forward."

"Abomination!" Ron all but hissed, and I agreed with him.

My head came up, and I squinted at the seraph, pleading, "The memory was so beautiful. I didn't want the black wings to eat it and have it be gone forever. I'd give it back if I could. Can you give it back to her for me?" Only now could I meet the angel's eyes, and I blinked at the understanding, no, the pleased expression it wore. "I gave them a part of my own soul instead, and they didn't know the difference," I added more confidently.

"I couldn't let that much joy be forgotten by . . . everyone."

"Mmmm." Again the thunder rumbled in a clear blue sky, and the sun rose higher. "You claimed her with ancient law, giving an equal sacrifice for her soul. There is no need to make repairs," it said, touching my shoulder in support, and I felt lifted, buoyed. "Memories grow with the sharing, as do souls. You took a memory of the future, not the present. She still has it. There is a long life for her now with much sorrow, and memories too beautiful to forget are what sustain us. The trick . . ." The seraph hesitated, its lips quirking in what had to be humor. ". . . is to recognize them."

I was almost in tears, but Ron was smug as he set his feet wide apart and crossed his arms over his chest in a confident manner. "Then Paul got her a guardian angel after all," he stated. "If she lives, then she must have her guardian. Good for Paul."

The angel let go of my shoulder and laughed. The sound pealed forth, shaking the air. Frightened, I wanted to run, but the angel was focused on Ron, not me.

"No!" it said, and a cool breeze touched my face, heavy with moisture, odd here in the desert. "But good for Paul, yes. Madison showed a lost soul how to recognize joy, and Paul's counsel gave her the strength to fight for it. Her fate is changing this very moment, and her life is lived, not endured. She dies with grace and touches many souls." The seraph turned to me as I stared, openmouthed. "You and Paul did well."

"Tammy is okay!" I said, elated. We'd done it. We'd done it twice! Surely they had to see now? But then my mood softened, ebbed, and died. Tammy's fate wasn't my only worry. Fingering my amulet, I thought of my body. I had said I'd give the amulet back if I ever found my body. I didn't want to. I wanted to stay. They'd let me stay if I wanted to, right?

"Tammy is okay," the seraph said, beaming warmth into me to make me feel good despite my world falling apart around me. "Because of you and Paul. Because you *worked together*."

Ron lost his confident stance, grim and ugly. "Paul is not going to succeed me," he said vehemently. "This is an outrage! Light and dark working together. It isn't done! I've served for a hundred lifetimes—"

"And you'll continue to do so," the seraph interrupted him, beautiful bare feet grinding the grit as the angel turned. "You are going to forget Paul's intentions and what has passed this morning."

My eyes widened as it raised Ron's sword over his head, and plunged it deep into the paving stones. The earth shook, and both Ron and I fell. He scrambled up, but I stayed where I was, feeling the air grow damp against me. Above us, thick rain clouds had formed. Rain in the desert, a gift out of time, out of place.

The angel stood before us, terrible in its beauty and anger. "Reclaim your sword to bring about heaven's will," it intoned, and Ron looked in horror at his blade sticking out of the patio like Excalibur. "Use the time before you find your bravery to reflect," the seraph added. "There is one last task for me before I leave this confused maelstrom of existence, and you are not required for it, Chronos."

I didn't understand why Ron was staring at me so hatefully, standing before his sword as if it was a snake. If he didn't reclaim it, his amulet wouldn't work at full strength.

"He takes it, and his memory of what Paul did this night is gone," the seraph said, crouching down to be at my level. It was an odd position for an angel, and my breath caught at his nearness.

Slowly I stood up, my eyebrows rising in understanding. "And if he leaves it there, he won't have the strength to stop us," I said, and the angel beamed, holding out a hand as it knelt before me.

I looked at it, feeling my face going cold. The seraph was asking for my amulet. "One last thing," it said, and I clutched at the stone.

"You want my amulet," I whispered, and Ron snorted, clearly not upset that I was going to lose everything as well.

"Yes." The seraph gracefully rose to a stand as well, still holding a hand out.

"But I proved fate can be changed, that a dying soul can be rekindled," I said, looking over the cooling desert as if my past deeds would be out there somewhere to find and collect, like pretty rocks. "All of us together, light and dark. We saved Tammy's soul and her life. I know I said I'd give it up when I found my body, but I saw what happened to those who are given guardian angels but aren't able to rekindle their souls on their own, and that is awful."

"Agreed," the seraph said. "The songs of the guardian angels did much to sway heaven."

"But to kill a person outright to save his or her soul," I lamented. "That is awful, too."

"Agreed," the seraph said again, a touch of impatience in its tone, a hand still outstretched. "Your amulet, please. It is confusing here. I want to leave."

"Give it to the angel, Madison, or it will take it," Ron said smugly, and my reach to pull it over my head almost stopped. I wanted to cry as I felt the amulet leave me, felt the bond between us stretch and hold. "Paul and I," I said as the seraph cupped its hands around it, hiding it from me. "We changed things. I can understand why I need to forget, but don't make him forget."

A glow leaked from between the seraph's fingers, pure and divine. The angel opened its hand, and my white-hot stone slowly cooled, shifting through the spectrum until it was again black. "We have no intention of making him forget," the seraph said, extending my amulet back to me.

I stared at it, unbelieving. *They are giving it back?*

"It took several hundred years of searching the time lines

to find someone able to manipulate time and have *the fate*, to make the choice he has made," the seraph said. "Here. Take your amulet. I want to leave."

I stared at my amulet, dangling from the seraph's fingers. *They're giving it back?*

Slowly I reached out, fingers closing on air an instant before I touched it. "B-but," I stammered as I looked at it still in the seraph's possession. "I found my body. Claimed it."

The seraph lowered its arm as Ron began to pace, his sword between us. "Do you want to be the dark timekeeper?" the seraph asked.

"Yes!" I exclaimed, looking at my amulet. "But I want to be alive, too!"

The seraph shrugged. "So you changed your mind," it said, smiling. "We knew you would. It was fated such. Take your amulet. It has been adjusted."

Not breathing, I reached out, hesitating.

"Take it!" the seraph thundered, and I jumped, grabbing it.

"There once was a girl named Madison," sang a familiar voice, and my eyes shot to the seraph's shoulder. It was Grace, and I could see her. I mean, really see her! She was beautiful, glowing with spiderwebs and dew. I couldn't seem to breathe, and she laughed, almost falling off the seraph's shoulder.

"Check out the time line," she suggested, and I closed my eyes, gasping. It was so clear, so precise, and tears pricked at my eyes. I could see everything intertwined, one thing affecting the other, until it was singing a glorious, resonant hum of existence. My dad was worried about me. Shoe was thinking of me, curious after having talked to Tammy. Josh was at home, sending me a worried text message. Wendy wasn't thinking about me at all—and that was okay. She was living her life . . . joyfully.

"I'm the dark timekeeper," I whispered, and my eyes flew open to see Grace beaming.

"You always have been," the seraph said, kneeling as if trying to get closer to my happiness. "But now you have the chance to be a person, too, to live as those you're trying to save. Even a superhero needs a place to be normal," it finished with a wry smile.

I sat on the tile and blinked. Far above us, the clouds thickened. It was raining, but the drops were evaporating before reaching the ground. I had my amulet. I had my body. They were going to let me do things my way. "Then you agree?" I said, needing to hear it. "No more scythings?"

Again the seraph laughed, an echo of thunder above following it. "The scythings will continue," it said, and Ron, standing before his sword with his hands fisted, grunted.

"But you agreed . . ." I started, not caring I was arguing with one of God's angels.

The seraph shifted, standing up to tower over me. "Your plans are sound. But, Madison, the reapers are a different drawer of spoons."

My shoulders slumped as Ron harrumphed. "Not so easy, Madison," he taunted, almost reaching for his sword, but not yet ready to consign his memory of Paul's intent to the crapper.

"Reapers serve their timekeepers out of respect," the seraph said, frowning at Ron's glee. "It is their . . . choice to change or not. The guardian angels are behind this shift as one, but the reapers?"

Depressed, I slumped on Ron's patio, hating his smile at me. "Then I've gained nothing," I whispered.

The seraph's touch was almost not there, it was so soft as it tilted my chin up to look me in the eye. Grace was behind it, smiling, and my head hurt at their combined beauty. "You've gained everything. You will work with reapers as they come to you seeking answers. And they will come seeking answers. Word of what has happened is echoing between heaven and earth. That you and Paul have worked together has reapers questioning. Both the light *and* dark. Light and dark, they will come to you, and light and dark, you will send them out together as one to save or damn souls. That's why we sent Demus to you. He has doubt. Your questions will be his answers."

My eyebrows rose. They had sent Demus to me because he might listen? "Then the cullings will stop?" I whispered.

But the seraph was shaking its head, smiling benevolently. "I told you, light and dark, you will pair them up, and light and dark, you will send them out. Together the reapers will try to change fate, but if it is determined that the soul will remain steadfast to ruin despite their efforts, a dark reaper will cull their soul, and a light reaper will weep."

"I don't understand," I stammered.

"The cullings will continue," the seraph insisted. "But it will be the light reaper who deems the soul lost, not the dark."

My mouth made an O of understanding. The light, who once assigned the guardian angels, would be less likely to write a soul off. A person would have to truly be beyond hope for that to happen. It was enough. This, I decided, I could do.

Seeing my resolve reflected in my eyes, the seraph nodded and drew back. "If a change can be made, then fate will intervene and a life will be lived. I hope this happens. It's up to you." The seraph smiled, and I almost burst with happiness. "And your reapers. There is no more using the ancient law, though. It worked this time, but you are not to risk yourself in such a way again. Understand?"

I exhaled, smiling wryly up at it. "This is the best I'm going to get, isn't it?"

The seraph arced its wings to touch over its head, an angel's version of a shrug I'd seen Barnabas do. It extended a hand for me, and feeling renewed, I slipped my hand among the angel's fingers as we turned to the sun.

A clear light filled me at the touch, thrilling me down to my toes. The desert vanished with a crack of real lightning. I gasped, and then felt myself go misty. The first patters of large, heavy drops of rain hit my face. I was both there to feel it, and gone, half of me feeling the warm plops of rain, and half the emptiness of nothing. And then the warm wetness vanished and I was nowhere.

I panicked, disembodied and unreal. I clutched at my amulet as if it could save me, but I wasn't sure I even had hands anymore.

A girl once dared walk the line, came Grace's thought into mine, and I grasped it. *Seeking union of soul and divine. Light and dark work together, for now, perhaps forever, but it's going to take eons of time.*

Eons of time, I mused, calming as I realized I was safe. I just wasn't sure where I was anymore. I felt my body seem to lift, finishing the move that the angel had started in the Arizona desert. I took a breath not knowing if it was real. It made my heart beat and my blood move.

A blinding light pulsed over me, and I cowered, my hand that had been in the seraph's grip falling to my side. Blinking, I brought my head up to see that I was standing in my room, not Ron's patio. My reflection stared back at me from my mirror, and Grace darted over everything as if she hadn't seen it in years. Numb, I stared at myself in that ridiculous black outfit. I looked tired, small, and really dirty.

Heart pounding, I turned, not believing it. I was home. Alive.

I looked down, the hand clenching my amulet falling open. And I still had my amulet.

"Now what?" I wondered aloud, peering into its depths to see sparkles and rainbows.

THIRTEEN

The mall was pleasantly busy, the weekend traffic moving quickly past the displayed photographs, most people not seeing them apart from being something to avoid on the way to a new pair of jeans or an iced mocha. But that was how we lived our lives, most times—unless something smacked us hard enough to realize that life is fleeting—too busy with the details of existence to recognize the things that turn existing into living. No, I wasn't depressed, just introspective, and as I stood before Nakita's photograph of a silent hospital at night, I hoped no one noticed the out-of-state plates. She'd taken it at a slant, then went on to blur it to make the lights glow and overtake everything, almost like what I saw in a far-distant flash forward. But still . . . if you looked close . . .

"Did she blur it intentionally?" my dad asked from behind

me, and I jumped, almost spilling the milk shake I was slamming down. Josh had gotten it for me before excusing himself to lurk in the nearby food court. He liked my photography, but after five minutes of it, he'd had his fill. Barnabas and Nakita were AWOL, but I figured they were around, avoiding my mother like most people. Yes, my mother. She had shown up unannounced this morning claiming to be here for the mall show, but I think she had been on her way to a California youth detention center and got diverted. *Thank you, God, Barnabas, seraphs, and maybe, Grace.*

"Gosh, I've no clue what's in Nakita's mind when she takes pictures," I said. "She just points and clicks. At everything."

"Yes, well, you used to be the same way," my dad goodnaturedly chided me as I rolled my eyes. His hand on my shoulder made me feel like I belonged, and I took it, tugging him away before he noticed the out-of-state plates. Neck craning, he tried to get a longer look.

"Whatever she's doing, she needs to keep doing it," he said, squinting behind him. "All her work has a unique . . . feral quality. It's as if I'm seeing sorrow, concern, or joy for the very first time through her."

"Really?"

"Yes, really," he said, then he did a double take. "That's not our local hospital, is it?"

"I hadn't noticed." Flustered, I stopped at Nakita's last entry, then had a mild panic attack. I hadn't seen this one—didn't even remember her taking it. It had won top honors according to the little sticker on the auction slip, but that's not what had me tense. The photograph was of me from the back as I walked down a dark sidewalk, head down and arms over my middle. It was Shoe's house at night, and there were orbs trailing behind me like bubbles. At least fifty. Crap, had there been guardian angels following me and I never even knew it?

"Um, you want to see mine?" I said, tugging on my dad's arm to get him to where my mother stood alone before my three entries, her trendy purse over an arm and her heels planted firmly on the scratched mall floor as if mine were the only photographs out here, but he didn't move, his eyes fixed on Nakita's black-and-white photograph of me with the angels.

"How did she do that?" he asked, finger hovering over the orbs. "And why? Two photos superimposed, you think?"

"Probably," I said, becoming more nervous. Had they been following me to evaluate me as a timekeeper? Barnabas seemed to think that for all their small size, guardian angels were more powerful than even the seraphs. Could be. Someone told me once that cherubs sat next to God's throne, but the more I heard from the "experts" the more I realized we didn't have a clue.

Slowly my dad's shoulders slumped and his eyes became sorrowful as he peered at the picture. I hesitated, and then, knowing that he wouldn't move until he satisfied his curiosity, I dropped back to stand with him and tried to see what he was looking at—not what was behind the glass, but what was in the mind of the person taking the picture.

The black-and-white threw everything into a misty sharpness, and it looked like the weight of the world was on me. I remembered that night. Nakita had perfectly captured my worry, the need to fix what I'd broken. And as I looked at it, that same tiredness seemed to soak into me again. Nakita was good. Really good.

"Has it been that hard?" my dad whispered, turning to me with a soft pain still in his gaze. "I thought you were happy here. If you want to go back with your mother . . ."

"No!" I quickly assured him, giving him a sideways hug and almost spilling my shake again. "I'm happy. I like it here. I like living with you. I feel . . . centered," I said, using one of his favorite words. "It was just a rough night. You know . . . boyfriends. But we're okay now." I glanced at Josh at the food court, then blinked. Barnabas had joined him. "I didn't even know she took it," I finished.

My dad was looking at my mother, who was standing before my photographs like they were the *Mona Lisa*. "If you're sure."

"One hundred percent," I said fervently, then added, "Just don't tell Mom, okay? She makes me wear funny clothes."

He laughed at that, looking at my short skirt, tights, and the top that was so uncoordinated with the rest that it worked. Much of the tension he'd adopted since finding out my mom was in town seemed to evaporate. He'd been looking at me all morning as if he was trying to figure out what was different. I think his subconscious knew I was alive again, and he was trying to find a more reasonable explanation as to what the change was. Smiling, he put an arm over my shoulder and we slowly moved toward my mom. I'd won an honorable mention, and it was at this one that my mother was standing, her pride radiating from her more than her three-hundred-dollar perfume.

"This is wonderful, Madison," she said, shunning the pen tied to the auction slip to use her own turquoise-inlaid pen to make an outrageous offer. "Still taking shots of daydreams?" she added, referring to my childhood preoccupation of photographing clouds. This one was nothing special, just a photograph to fulfill a class requirement. It didn't deserve even an honorable mention as far as I was concerned. The one I'd taken of the black wings circling an abandoned house hadn't even placed.

"Thanks, Mom," I said, giving her equal hug-time so they wouldn't start arguing. I pressed into her, my eyes closing at the scent of raw silk. Her grip on me seemed a shade too tight, a moment too long, and she seemed concerned when I broke from her and she searched my gaze. She looked the same in her fashionable shoes, her creased slacks, and her silk blouse. Her hair was in the latest conservative cut, and her makeup was perfect. She had huffed as usual at my choice of clothes and Dad's casual slacks and shirt, but I could tell she was worried about me. The wrinkles around her eyes had broken free of her expensive cream to give her away.

"I can't believe you came up all the way from Florida for a

mall show, Mom," I said, trying to get her to stop looking at Barnabas and Josh.

Her attention came back to me, and a quick, unsure smile flashed across her. "And miss this? Not going to happen. I didn't have anything this week but a cancer fund-raiser, and the people running it know better than me what needs to be done." She put her pen away, carefully ignoring my dad as she moved to the picture with the black wings.

"Did I tell you they had me changing planes in Arizona?" my mother added, shaking her head at the "crows." "The connecting flight was canceled. I almost got on a flight to San Diego, not Illinois. Hell of a way to run an airline."

I fidgeted, not knowing what to say. "Well, I'm glad you're here," I finally said. "It really means a lot to me." I slurped the last of my shake, seeing my dad hide a smile as my mom frowned at the rude noise. It was the first time in months that I'd eaten anything in front of him without duress. I was still hungry, too, and I glanced at the nearby food court where Barnabas waited with Josh and a half-eaten plate of fries. Nakita had shown up, standing with her hip cocked and her eyes narrowed. She and Barnabas were arguing. Big surprise.

My mother, ever sensitive to the boys around her one and only daughter, raised her eyebrows at the incongruous trio. Barnabas was eye candy to the max, but it was Josh who was watching me with hopeful eyes, even as he stuffed fries in his mouth. My stomach rumbled. It seemed like it was making up for lost time. At least my bruises didn't show.

"Hey, um, you guys mind if I go talk to my friends for a minute?" I asked, wanting some of those fries before Josh ate them all.

"Yes, go," my mother said, frowning suspiciously at Barnabas. "They're invited to come with us for lunch," she added, her gaze rising to linger on my amulet.

"I'll ask." I was backing up, and I flushed when my dad shook his wrist, then adjusted his watch.

"Reservations at twelve thirty," my mother added. "I think the van I rented will hold all of us. I'd like to meet your new friends." She looked at her watch and murmured, "Eleven seventeen, Bill." Looking up with an exhale, she said to me, "Especially your boyfriends."

Oh, God. Just take me now. "You've met Josh," I said guardedly, knowing she was talking about Barnabas.

"Who is that other young man talking to Nicki?" she asked.

"It's Nakita," I corrected her, growing uncomfortable as Nakita seemed to deflate at something Barnabas said, the reaper's anger washing away to leave only sadness. Something was going on. Josh, too, looked unhappy.

"And Barnabas isn't my boyfriend," I said, my mouth dropping open as Nakita gave Barnabas a hug. "He's more like . . ." I hesitated, blinking as Nakita turned and walked away, head down and looking miserable. "He's helped me with a few issues," I said, my voice preoccupied. *What on earth is going on?*

My mother cleared her throat, and I turned, flushing at her unbelieving gaze. "He seems to be quite the Casanova."

When my mother got it wrong, she really got it wrong. "Yea-a-a-ah," I said, just wanting to go over and find out what was up. "Um, would you mind if I, uh . . ."

"Go!" my dad said, finding his own Bic pen in a pocket and topping my mother's offer on my lackluster photograph. My mother huffed as I was turning away. I couldn't help my smile. I knew that there wasn't a chance that they would ever get back together again, but there was a peace that hadn't been there before, and it was nice to have them both around me. Centered, as my dad would say.

Head down as I lived for a moment in my tiny daydream, I tossed my empty shake cup away, feeling good as I joined Barnabas and Josh. Running a fry through his ketchup, Josh gave me an understanding grin as he took in my folks, one comfortable and almost sloppy, the other uptight and proper.

"Madison, your mom looks . . . nice?" he offered, and I snorted.

"I can't imagine why you and your mother didn't get along," Josh added, and I slumped into my chair.

"She's okay," I said, pulling myself upright so my mom wouldn't frown. "She just wants to be sure I'm safe."

I reached for one of Josh's fries, and he pushed the plate to me. A warm spot grew in my middle, and I smiled. Yeah, he liked me. A guy wouldn't just give up his fries like that if he didn't.

Barnabas brought his gaze back from the shop that Nakita had gone into, his expression cross. "I can't go for lunch," he said irately.

My eyebrows went up. "You heard that?"

Josh squirted more ketchup out. "He heard your entire conversation. Sitting with him is like sitting with an FBI agent. I, though, would like to go to lunch." He ate a fry, narrowly escaping dripping ketchup on himself. "I already cleared it with my mom," he added, mouth full.

I followed Barnabas's dark gaze down the hall. He was brooding about Nakita. "I, ah, talked to Paul this morning," I said, and Barnabas jerked his attention back to me. A trace of what might be alarm drifted through him, and I put up a hand.

"We're good," I said. "Ron pulled his sword out of his patio and he doesn't remember anything about Paul helping us last night."

"Good, good." Barnabas's words weren't quite jiving with his body language. "I heard from Paul, too," he added, eyes on the table.

"Really?" I hoped Nakita was okay. It wasn't like her to just . . . leave like that. She'd been on cloud nine, maybe literally, since finding out that I'd retained my timekeeper position and that things had the potential to change.

The silence brought my attention back to the table. Josh was giving Barnabas a look, and the reaper was studiously ignoring him, gazing at his amulet. The usually flat stone was glowing, and I saw the hint of yellow in it. As in shifting to red, yellow.

"What's going on?" I asked, remembering Nakita's angry, then sad mood.

"Just tell her, Barney," Josh prompted him, earning a glare from the reaper.

"Tell me what?" I demanded.

Still, Barnabas sat there with his lips pressed tight, hands clasped tightly on the table. I could see my mother beyond him, watching us.

Josh slurped some of his drink. "Barnabas wants to go back to Ron," he said flatly.

My lips parted, and I sat up straight. "Excuse me?"

My loud exclamation had caught my mom's attention, but my dad caught her elbow and tugged her away, giving us the privacy that I deserved but she didn't understand.

"Ron?" I said softer, but no less vehemently.

Barnabas's expression had gone from defiant to miserable. Dark eyes pleading, he reached for my hands, and I pulled them away. No wonder Nakita was pissed.

"It's not like that," he said, "and I don't want to go back *to* Ron. I want to go back *with* Paul."

Paul?

Seeing my anger hesitate, Barnabas leaned in. "Madison, I talked to Paul this morning after the seraph tuned your amulet.

He says that not only does Ron not remember him helping us but that Ron doesn't remember me leaving him, either. Ron thinks I'm still a light reaper in good standing. Why do you think the seraph did that?"

"You want to go back?" I said, hating that my voice was so high. "You don't think we can do this? After I convinced the seraphs to let us try?"

"No!" He shook his head, glancing at Josh, who was getting a chuckle at his expense. "I do believe. But so does Paul. He wants to help, and he can't do it on his own. He needs someone to run interference for him, like Josh does with you."

Josh grinned, shoving a fry into his mouth. "I'm your secret agent backup," he said, clearly enjoying himself.

I slumped, elbows on the table.

"You've got Nakita to help you, too," Barnabas said softly, his head almost touching mine. "Paul doesn't have anyone. I've known Ron his entire life, and it's going to take that kind of knowledge to work around him. Paul is going to be sending you light reapers, and someone is going to have to lie to Ron about it." He grinned softly, leaning back with a sly look. "If there's one thing I can do, it's lie. I've been lying to myself for eons. I'll be there if you need me, but meantime, I'll stay with Paul and watch for the light reapers who might be looking for new answers to old questions, and then cover for those who do."

My heart was aching. "Okay," I said, feeling the lump in my throat start to grow. He was still leaving, but he was leaving with purpose. Barnabas was going to be light and dark both. He could do it. To ask him to stay would be selfish. "I'm going to miss you," I said, refusing to even let my eyes tear up, much less cry.

"Hey!" he said, his light touch on my hand seeming to warm me. "We can still talk, right?"

I nodded, miserable, though I had everything I wanted. Barnabas had been with me from the moment I had woken up dead in the morgue, and saying good-bye was like . . . breaking up, sort of.

Barnabas stood, and I blinked up at him. "It's not like I'm dying," he said as he leaned down to give me a hug. "But I'm going to miss the way you used to scramble to look like you just got out of bed in the morning."

My eyes closed, and I could feel the divine in him, smelling like feathers and sunflowers. My thoughts went to Sarah, living her life with him. What would it be like, I wondered, to have the divine with you all the time? It would be too much for me, and I let him go.

He pulled himself to his full height, and I smiled up at him. "She loved you to her last breath, didn't she?" I said suddenly.

Barnabas hesitated, scrambling until he figured out I was talking about Sarah. "And beyond," he said seriously. "Some-times . . . I envy you with your endings. Endings are not always bad. Most times, they're just beginnings in disguise." He inclined his head, gaze going past me. "I should go."

Josh wiped his hand and extended his fist. "Catch you on the flip side, birdman," he said, and the two banged knuckles.

The lump in my throat seemed to settle in for good, and I took a deep breath. If my mother saw me like this, she'd think that I was crushing on Barnabas.

"And anyway," Barnabas said as he turned to leave, "I think you're going to be too busy to miss me."

I followed his gaze down the hallway to where Nakita stood, confident and sassy again with Demus beside her. The dark reaper seemed embarrassed, but the light in his eyes demanded answers that he could find only with me.

My lips parted, and I looked at Barnabas, grinning as he spun in a slow half circle, the hem of his duster furling.

Josh grunted as he crushed his plate and napkin into a ball. "I think Nakita has brought you your first turncoat," he said, and I just shook my head, seeing the belligerent confusion in the redheaded angel standing beside Nakita.

I stood, thinking this afternoon with my parents was going to be memorable if nothing else. Good thing Nakita could change memories. "Do you think he eats seafood?" I asked Josh.

"Beats me."

Barnabas was leaving, but Demus seemed to be taking his place. Bringing another reaper around to a colorful frame of mind might be fun, seeing as he was looking for answers. I had my body, and my amulet, and a future that was going to be both challenging and rewarding as I worked one-on-one with heaven's own, showing them what the collective consciousness of humanity had distilled into me—that life was as important as the soul, and to end one to save the other wasn't necessary if light and dark could work together to bring about understanding.

Light and dark, I thought, fingering my amulet. Good and bad, soul and body, all together in a mixed-up mess that somehow made divine sense. Perfectly satisfied, I walked beside Josh, wondering what tomorrow would be, what souls I might save. Today, though, I was me, going out for lunch with my parents and my friends.

And that was just fine with me.